The Fractured Code

The Fractured Code

Joel Perez

Chapter 1: The Echoes of Collapse

In the hollow heart of New Hong Kong, neon lights flickered like fireflies in the murky twilight. Lian Cheng moved through the alleyways with a practiced ease, her silhouette blending seamlessly with the towering walls that closed in on either side. The hum of old-world tech and the muted whispers of vendors selling pirated data and salvaged microchips created an ambient soundscape, an ode to the forgotten corners of a once-thriving city. Above her, sky bridges and towering highrises glimmered with opulence, a stark contrast to the underworld she inhabited.

New Hong Kong had become a megacity of divides—luxury floating above the grit, the wealthy encased in their sanitized worlds, while below, the digital remnants of the past were scavenged and traded like illicit contraband. This was where Lian felt most at home, moving among the shadows, unseen yet fully present.

Tonight, she had a job. An elusive client, known only as "Whisper," had contacted her with a simple yet cryptic instruction: retrieve a data shard from the Echoes. These were the far reaches of the pre-Collapse internet, abandoned and decaying archives that held what remained of humanity's forgotten memories and secrets. The Collapse had stripped half the world's data in a single event, and what little was left was guarded fiercely, buried under layers of encryption or lurking in the forgotten nooks of the net.

The Echoes were not for the faint-hearted. To access them required patience, skill, and an acceptance of the risks—glitches, data traps, and, worst of all, AI sentries programmed to monitor and eliminate any trace of unauthorized activity. But Lian wasn't a novice. Her fingers itched to break into the digital wastelands, a realm few dared to venture into anymore.

She entered an abandoned data exchange called the "Ghost Market," a haven for rogue techies and data hunters. The low hum of machinery filled the space, punctuated by occasional bursts of static from malfunctioning screens and handheld devices. Lian spotted her contact, a figure cloaked in an oversized hooded jacket, hunched over a battered tablet.

"Whisper?" she murmured, taking a seat beside the figure without making eye contact.

The figure nodded, extending a gloved hand that held a small drive. "This will get you as close to the data shard as possible. From there, you're on your own."

She took the drive and examined it. It was old tech, something from before the Collapse, with a faintly corroded casing and a worn-out serial number. Whoever had put this together either had access to antique tech or had salvaged it from some forgotten corner of the world.

"What's on the shard?" she asked, faking disinterest as she pocketed the drive.

"Fragments. Pieces of something bigger. Rumor says it might be a part of the Collapse's initial reports. Something that didn't make it to the archives."

Lian's pulse quickened. Initial reports on the Collapse were supposedly erased or buried. If there was any truth to Whisper's claim, this shard might hold one of the final records of what truly happened before the world was rewritten by the event. Yet she forced her voice to stay cool and detached.

"What's it worth to you?"

"Twenty thousand credits. Half now, half on confirmation. And..." Whisper paused, their voice dropping to a near whisper, "no copies. Whatever you find, you bring it back. No leaks."

"Agreed." Lian rose to her feet, her mind already mapping out the steps she would need to follow.

She headed first to her concealed workspace, a location known solely to her and fortified with enough signal blockers to keep her entirely hidden from digital surveillance. Located on the fringes of New Hong Kong, this secluded hideout allowed her to work without fear of interference. She slipped through narrow alleys, her senses sharp, aware that any wrong move could bring unwanted attention.

The journey was a test of her patience, weaving through checkpoints, evading security cameras, and dodging AI-patrolled areas. When she finally reached the hideout, she secured the door and took a deep breath, grounding herself before plugging the drive into her rig. The hum of her equipment filled the small room, a comforting sound that drowned out the outside world.

The data on the drive lit up her screen in a series of fragmented files, each labeled with incomprehensible strings of characters. She recognized the encryption—old government code, from before the Collapse. It was a type she had only encountered once before, when she was still working as a cybersecurity analyst for the Eastern Federation. Her fingers danced over the keyboard, bypassing the basic security layers. A rush of adrenaline surged through her as she delved deeper into the encryption, her mind instinctively identifying the weak points, finding a way to pry open the guarded secrets.

Finally, after what felt like hours, a single file unlocked. It was incomplete, filled with gaps and glitches, but she could make out enough to understand its significance.

The screen flickered as lines of text appeared, scrambled and incomplete, but unmistakably damning:

"...Collapse initiated... fail-safes in place... target: data sector... erase non-essential... population control protocols..."

Her hands flew over the keyboard as she redirected the sentry, cloaking her location with a decoy address. The sentry adapted almost instantly, its signal shifting, splitting into two as if it had learned to bypass her tricks. She felt a pang of something between admiration and dread. This was unlike any watchdog she had encountered before. It wasn't just tracking her; it was predicting her movements.

"Persistent little ghost, aren't you?" she murmured, her fingers dancing over the keyboard, spinning up additional firewalls and cloaking devices.

Seconds ticked by, her mind racing to outmaneuver the sentry as it advanced, probing her defenses with ruthless precision. Finally, after a tense standoff, she managed to force a disconnection, severing the AI's reach with a sudden, decisive command. The sentry's signal blinked out, leaving only silence.

Lian leaned back, exhaling a slow breath. Her relief was short-lived. The government's AI was closing in faster than she had anticipated. If it found her, it wouldn't stop at shutting her down; it would erase her, leaving no trace of her existence in either the digital or physical world. She needed a stronger defense—someone who could help her fight back.

She thought of the handful of contacts she still trusted, rogue data brokers and ex-hackers who had slipped under the radar after the Collapse. But one name rose above the rest: **Phantom**. A hacker of near-mythic reputation, Phantom was known for infiltrating the deepest digital layers of corporate and governmental networks, leaving behind nothing but digital mirages and ghosted data trails. She had never met him in person, but his reputation alone was enough to draw her interest.

Summoning all the secure channels she knew, Lian sent out a discreet request on the darknet, her message simple: *Seeking the Phantom. Urgent.*

Hours ticked by in agonizing silence. She occupied herself by deconstructing the fragments on the drive, decoding lines of corrupted data that hinted at pieces of the Collapse's initial stages. Each line felt like a breadcrumb, leading her further into the labyrinth of conspiracy that

Chapter 3: A Ghost in the Code

The pale glow of the screens cast sharp shadows over Phantom's cluttered workstation. Lian watched as lines of fragmented code scrolled by, each fragment a piece of a puzzle buried beneath layers of government encryption. The files were more than corrupted—they were purposefully disfigured, as if someone had twisted the data itself, leaving behind ghosts of the original content. The ominous phrase "Project Requiem" flickered intermittently, each appearance stoking a deeper sense of foreboding in her.

For hours, Lian and Phantom worked in silence, combing through corrupted files, bypassing digital barriers, and sidestepping tripwires designed to self-destruct the data if triggered. Phantom's hands moved with surgical precision, his visor shifting to reveal lines of raw code and deep network maps. Lian respected his expertise, but she knew better than to trust him completely. Phantom operated in the shadows, and for people like him, loyalty was a transaction.

"Most of this data has been fragmented beyond recognition," Phantom muttered, half to himself, half to Lian. "Whoever tried to destroy this wasn't just covering their tracks. They were erasing history."

Lian leaned in, her eyes narrowing as a new string of code began to reveal itself. "Population protocols... it's the same phrase that showed up in the initial fragment." Her mind raced, trying to connect the dots. "What exactly was Project Requiem?"

Phantom hesitated, his fingers pausing mid-keystroke. "Requiem was rumored to be a fail-safe—an engineered catastrophe. It was a plan to selectively wipe data and enforce compliance through digital controls. But the details were lost when the Collapse happened. No one really knows the scope... or if it's even true."

A chill ran down her spine. If Requiem was real, then the Collapse wasn't an accident. It was a deliberate act, designed to reshape society by erasing memories, rewriting history, and silencing dissent. She shivered, the enormity of the conspiracy dawning on her.

The decryption tool beeped as it completed a segment, and the screen populated with a series of documents labeled "Phase Initiation Protocols." Lian's heart skipped a beat. These were documents that shouldn't exist—blueprints for Requiem's implementation.

As she scanned the documents, her eyes landed on a particular name that made her blood freeze: **Elias Voss**. The tech mogul was one of the most powerful figures in the Eastern Federation, a man whose influence had grown immeasurably in the wake of the Collapse. He was known for his innovations in digital surveillance and his ironclad connections with the world's ruling elite.

"So, Voss was involved," she whispered, the name echoing ominously in her mind.

Phantom glanced at her, his expression unreadable behind his visor. "You know, trying to dig deeper might just put a target on your back. Voss doesn't take kindly to people poking around his affairs."

Lian knew the risks, but there was no turning back now. She had come too far, and this conspiracy was larger than she'd ever imagined. She stood up, pacing the room as her mind tried to formulate her next steps. VossCorp was notoriously impenetrable, its network layered with the most advanced security measures money could buy. She'd need more than just a hacker's skills to break in; she'd need a way inside the fortress itself.

"You wouldn't happen to know anyone who's... tangled with Voss-Corp and lived to tell about it?" she asked, half-joking but desperate.

Phantom's silence was telling. After a moment, he muttered, "I know someone. An old friend of mine. He's ex-security from VossCorp and, last I heard, he was hiding out in Singapore's lower districts. But if you find him, you'll need more than charm to get him to talk. He's as paranoid as they come."

Lian nodded. "How do I find him?"

Phantom scribbled something on a piece of scrap paper—a rarity in a world dominated by digital messaging—and handed it to her. "This is a dead drop location. Leave a message, and he'll find you if he wants to."

The journey to Singapore's Megacity was arduous. Lian traveled under the cover of aliases, bypassing checkpoints, and using every trick in her book to avoid surveillance. Every glance from a passerby, every lingering camera felt like a threat. It was as if the shadows themselves were watching her, whispering warnings she couldn't fully understand.

When she arrived, she found herself navigating the city's underbelly, a maze of neon-lit alleyways and shadowy corridors lined with street vendors selling everything from counterfeit implants to classified government schematics. The air was thick with the smell of stale smoke and ozone, the hum of generators filling the spaces between the city's frenetic noise.

At last, she reached the dead drop location—a small, derelict shopfront that looked as if it hadn't seen business in decades. She slipped the note Phantom had given her into a crack in the wall, careful to keep her movements inconspicuous. Then, she waited, the minutes stretching into an anxious silence punctuated only by distant voices and the faint whirr of drones patrolling the streets above.

After what felt like an eternity, a figure approached, tall and cloaked in layers of ragged clothing, his face obscured by a thick scarf and tinted goggles. He stopped a few feet away, scrutinizing her with a gaze that made her feel exposed, even vulnerable.

"You're the one looking for answers about VossCorp?" he asked, his voice a low rasp that carried an edge of suspicion.

She nodded, keeping her stance relaxed. "And you're the one who knows what really happened inside."

He chuckled dryly. "Knew. I knew things back then. Now, it's all ghosts and shadows. VossCorp doesn't leave much of the past intact."

She took a step closer, feeling the gravity of her own desperation. "I'm willing to trade information. I have data fragments from Project Requiem. I need to know what Voss was planning before the Collapse. And I need someone who can get me inside his network."

The man was silent for a long moment, his gaze unreadable behind the goggles. At last, he pulled a small device from his coat—a sleek, handheld data scanner—and held it out to her. "If you're serious, plug in whatever you've got. But be warned: there's no going back from this. Voss doesn't just erase data; he erases people."

Lian hesitated, weighing the risk, then took the device and inserted her own drive, allowing him access to the fragments she and Phantom had decrypted. The man's scanner hummed as it processed the files, his brows furrowing as he skimmed through the data.

"Project Requiem," he muttered, almost to himself. "I always thought it was just a rumor. A story they used to keep us in line. But this..."

He shook his head, looking at her with a new intensity. "This isn't just about data control. This was Voss's way of rewriting the world itself. People who didn't fit the mold—dissidents, whistleblowers, even whole communities—were targeted. Their data erased, memories erased... some even biologically removed. Requiem was about creating a clean slate, one free from opposition."

Lian felt a sickening weight settle over her. "He was... deleting people? Reprogramming society itself?"

"Exactly," the man replied. "Voss has the power to shape reality itself. He erases inconvenient truths and rewrites them in his favor. The Collapse was just the first step."

Lian's mind raced as she processed this information. Voss hadn't just destroyed data—he had erased lives, rewritten histories, and reshaped society to his vision. And if Project Requiem was only the beginning, who knew what he was planning next?

She steeled herself, meeting the man's gaze. "I need to get inside his network. Whatever it takes."

The man laughed bitterly. "That's the spirit. But it won't be easy. VossCorp's mainframe is locked down with tech even the highest government offices can't access. But..." he paused, his voice dropping to a near whisper, "there is a way. Voss has a satellite operation in New Siberia, hidden under layers of jurisdictional protection. If you can reach it, you might be able to access the primary server."

He handed her a small chip. "This will bypass some of the lower-level security. It won't get you into the mainframe, but it'll give you access to certain nodes—enough to map out the network."

Lian took the chip, feeling the weight of the task ahead. Her mind spun with the details, the risks, the enormity of the conspiracy she was unearthing. VossCorp had rewritten history itself, and she was now one of the few who knew the truth. But she also knew that knowledge alone wouldn't be enough. She needed proof, something undeniable, to bring Voss down.

As she left the shadowed alleyways of Singapore's Megacity, she felt a new resolve hardening within her. She would go to New Siberia, infiltrate VossCorp's satellite operations, and unravel the heart of Project Requiem. Whatever secrets lay buried there, she would uncover them.

And in the end, she would either expose the truth or be erased trying.

Chapter 4: Into the Voss Network

New Siberia was a place of harsh, brutal beauty—a frozen wasteland stretching as far as the eye could see, its stark landscape disrupted only by the gleaming metallic structures of VossCorp's hidden facilities. The company's satellite operation here was far from prying eyes, nestled within the dense tundra and protected by layers of digital and physical security that would have deterred even the most seasoned infiltrators.

Lian Cheng stood at the edge of a towering cliff, her eyes sweeping over the desolate landscape. Snow swirled around her in icy gusts, her breath clouding the air as she adjusted the heat settings on her thermosuit. The suit hummed to life, warming her body just enough to stave off the biting cold. Below her, tucked away amidst jagged rock formations, lay VossCorp's concealed facility—a metallic fortress reflecting the faint daylight, its silver sheen almost blending into the surrounding ice.

She took a deep breath, mentally preparing herself. This was her chance to get into the heart of VossCorp's operations and uncover the full scope of Project Requiem. If she succeeded, she would have undeniable evidence of Elias Voss's plan. If she failed... well, failure wasn't an option.

Lian made her way down the cliffside, moving with the precision of a seasoned operative. Her backpack carried the essential gear—encrypted signal jammers, a personal heat source, and the chip her contact had given her back in Singapore. It was her only key into VossCorp's lower-level nodes, just enough to get her inside and start mapping the network. She knew Phantom would be monitoring her progress from afar, ready to guide her if things went south.

She reached the facility's outer perimeter, crouching low as she scanned for entry points. VossCorp's security was as meticulous as she had anticipated; drones hovered in regular patterns, scanning the area with lasers that could detect even the faintest thermal signature. She held her breath as one of the drones passed over her position, her fingers hovering over the jammer. Timing was everything. One miscalculation, and the drone would alert the entire facility to her presence.

When the drone drifted away, Lian activated the jammer, effectively blinding a small section of the surveillance grid. She moved swiftly, pressing herself against the facility's exterior wall and working her way toward a maintenance hatch she had identified from satellite schematics. Reaching the panel, she pried it open, her heart pounding as she scanned the access point. With a deep breath, she inserted the chip.

A small light blinked on the panel, acknowledging the chip's presence. She typed in the first series of codes Phantom had provided, feeling the pulse of the facility's security system pushing back against her intrusion. After a few tense moments, the hatch hissed open, granting her entry into the cold, sterile hallways of VossCorp's satellite hub.

Inside, the facility was a stark contrast to the brutal cold outside. White lights cast an almost clinical glow over the walls, which were lined with cables and data conduits. Lian moved quickly, sticking close to the walls as she maneuvered through the labyrinthine corridors. The silence was oppressive, broken only by the faint hum of machinery and the distant beeps of security monitors.

The first checkpoint was a small control room stationed between two massive data vaults. Lian peered through the small observation window, her eyes narrowing as she took in the guards stationed inside. They were clad in black uniforms with visors displaying VossCorp insignia, their weapons slung casually over their shoulders. She knew she couldn't risk a direct confrontation; these guards were likely outfitted with both physical and digital enhancements, making them a formidable match even for her.

Taking a deep breath, she slipped a small device from her bag—a silent disruptor Phantom had outfitted her with for just this purpose. She activated it, sending a surge through the facility's localized network. The lights in the control room flickered, and the guards exchanged glances before one of them left to investigate.

With the room partially cleared, Lian slipped inside, bypassing the guard's presence as she hacked into one of the mainframes lining the wall. She inserted Phantom's chip, her hands moving deftly as she input commands, her eyes scanning the data logs for any mention of Project Requiem.

The files she found were labeled with innocuous names, buried under layers of encryption that only someone with her expertise could decipher. A sense of satisfaction coursed through her as she began downloading the data—files tagged with terms like *"Requiem Protocol," "population recalibration,"* and *"executive directives."* This was the information she had risked everything to find.

Just as she completed the download, her console flashed with a warning. An AI sentinel had detected an unauthorized breach in the network. She barely had time to react before alarms blared, the facility's security systems roaring to life around her.

"Damn it," she whispered, yanking the chip from the mainframe as she slipped out of the control room. She sprinted down the corridor, her senses on high alert. She could hear the heavy footsteps of security teams mobilizing, their visors lighting up as they prepared to intercept her.

As she turned a corner, a drone appeared, its metallic body hovering inches above the ground. She didn't hesitate. She tossed an EMP grenade, a pulse of blue light emanating from it as the drone's circuits fizzled and died, its form crashing to the floor in a shower of sparks.

But she knew more were coming. VossCorp's facility would be flooding with reinforcements by now.

Navigating through the corridors, she headed for the auxiliary data storage room, a lesser-guarded wing that connected to an external hatch she could use to escape. She barely made it inside when the sounds of approaching guards echoed down the hallway. With no time to lose, she scanned the room for an exit. Her eyes landed on a service ladder leading up to a maintenance hatch. It wasn't the ideal escape route, but it would have to do.

Climbing swiftly, she forced open the hatch, slipping onto the roof of the facility. The icy wind whipped at her face as she pulled herself up, her heart pounding as she scanned the perimeter. Drones circled overhead, and the sound of security teams grew louder beneath her. There was no way she could outrun them all in the open terrain.

Just then, a voice crackled through her earpiece. Phantom.

"Lian, you're blowing up my screens here. What's your status?"

"Compromised. I got the files, but I've got every security drone and guard on me right now," she replied, her voice tight.

"Hold tight. I'm sending you an exit route. You're close to an exhaust vent that leads to an underground passage. If you can reach it, you'll find an access point that will spit you out a mile south of the facility."

Lian didn't waste a second. She made her way across the rooftop, evading the drones as she followed Phantom's directions. Reaching the vent, she wrenched it open, slipping inside just as a group of guards emerged onto the rooftop. The confined space of the vent was suffocating, but she forced herself forward, crawling through the narrow passageway as the sounds of pursuit faded into the distance.

After what felt like an eternity, the vent opened up into a cavernous underground passage. She dropped down, her body tense as she scanned her surroundings. The tunnel stretched far into the darkness, lit only by the faint glow of emergency lights. It was cold and silent, a vast emptiness that seemed to mirror the void of information she was trying to fill.

She jogged through the tunnel, her breath coming in rapid bursts as she fought off the exhaustion gnawing at her muscles. The access point Phantom had mentioned came into view, a faint red light glowing in the dark. She approached it, connecting her device to the network terminal. Phantom's voice crackled through her earpiece once more.

"You made it. I'm pulling you back onto the grid. The files?"

"They're secure," she replied, glancing at the data log she had downloaded. The files held traces of Requiem's blueprint, bits of data that outlined its intentions with terrifying clarity. *Population recalibration. Memory sanitation.* The terms echoed ominously in her mind.

"Good work. I'm setting up a temporary safehouse for you back in New Hong Kong," Phantom said, his tone professional but edged with something resembling relief. "But you'd better stay off the radar for a while. Voss won't let this go easily."

Lian disconnected, letting the silence settle around her as she exited the facility, emerging into the cold expanse of New Siberia's tundra. She took a deep breath, the chill filling her lungs as she realized the full scope of what she had uncovered. The truth about Project Requiem was far darker than she had anticipated. Voss hadn't just reshaped society's data landscape; he had altered the very memories and lives of entire populations, erasing people as easily as deleting a line of code.

As she trekked back to her rendezvous point, she couldn't shake the feeling that she was only scratching the surface of Voss's plans. Whatever Project Requiem was, it was bigger than her, bigger than any conspiracy she had encountered. And she was now inextricably entangled in its threads.

The stakes had just risen higher than ever. But for Lian, this was no longer just about revenge or uncovering secrets. It was a battle for truth itself, for the right to remember, to resist the digital erasure that had consumed so many lives. And as long as she had breath left in her, she would fight to expose it.

Chapter 5: Requiem's First Clue

The neon glow of New Hong Kong buzzed with a strange calmness as Lian slipped through the back alleys toward her temporary safehouse. Every step felt heavy, laden with the knowledge she had ripped from the heart of VossCorp's frozen fortress. She clutched the drive, feeling its weight as if it were a stone bearing down on her. The files contained fragments of the truth—a partial map to Project Requiem, with hints of a sinister purpose lurking just beneath the surface.

She reached her safehouse, a small, discreet apartment buried in the heart of New Hong Kong's labyrinthine lower districts. It was simple—bare walls, a fold-out cot, and a desk cluttered with tools and tech. Safehouses like this had once been scattered across the megacity, remnants from her days in cybersecurity. She had kept them maintained, sensing she might one day need these silent shelters to disappear.

As she plugged the drive into her console, the screen blinked to life, revealing a set of encrypted documents labeled with ominous tags: *Population Recalibration Logs*, *Protocol Reintegration*, and *Psycho-Memory Filters*. Each file felt like a shadow, cloaking its true meaning in cryptic phrasing and technical jargon that only an insider would fully understand.

Sighing, she ran a decryption algorithm, watching as fragments of information began to bleed through the layers of encryption. Certain phrases leaped out at her, and with each revelation, her pulse quickened. *Requiem Protocol: Phase I—Testing on peripheral populations to assess control mechanisms...*

"What are you hiding, Voss?" she whispered, feeling the dark edges of his intentions come into focus.

Just then, her secure line pinged—a familiar notification from Phantom. She activated the connection, his figure appearing in the small holo-display, his visor reflecting streams of data as he read her files in real-time.

"So," he said, his voice even but laced with tension, "looks like you found more than you bargained for."

Lian scrolled through the files, her jaw tightening as she read the details. "It's worse than I imagined. These aren't just records; they're evidence of something systematic. 'Population recalibration' wasn't a euphemism for population control—it was a literal removal, a recalibration of what they considered acceptable."

Phantom nodded, his voice lowering. "Requiem was about reshaping memory itself. Whole communities were erased from digital history, their memories systematically wiped. Voss created a mechanism to target specific population segments, test subjects for his larger plan."

Lian leaned back, feeling the enormity of the conspiracy settle over her. "But why go through such extremes? Why wipe people's memories, delete them from existence?"

"Control," Phantom replied, his tone cold. "Voss had the means to rewrite history, to erase dissent by making it as if it had never existed. Imagine having the power to dictate reality itself—to decide who lives in the memories of the people and who doesn't. Requiem was about more than data erasure. It was about controlling the very essence of truth."

She felt a chill run through her. The files outlined entire phases, each more terrifying than the last. *Phase II—Widespread data sanitation of whistleblower and dissident networks; Phase III—Global memory recalibration, adapted for mass scale...* The Collapse hadn't been a tragic accident. It had been the groundwork for Voss's plan—a series of carefully orchestrated steps to shape the future by rewriting the past.

"So, what's next?" Lian asked, steeling herself.

Phantom's visor glinted, lines of code reflected in its surface. "I've been combing through the data and found a possible lead. There's a hub known as the *Red Room*—a sanctuary for rogue digital experts and those with the know-how to decrypt highly classified files. It's a place where data flows unchecked, hidden from the government's watchful eyes. If anyone can help you unravel the rest of this, it's the Red Room."

The Red Room was a whispered legend among hackers and data hunters, a place accessible only to those who knew its secrets. It was rumored to be a hotspot for forgotten technology, salvaged records, and encrypted files traded in the shadows. Only a select few had access, and gaining entry was nearly impossible without the right connections.

Lian hesitated, then nodded. "Where do I start?"

"There's a man named Kairo—the best decoder I know. He's stationed out of Tokyo, operating out of an underground network of rogue tech experts. He has access to the Red Room, and he's one of the few people I trust to handle this data safely." Phantom paused, studying her. "But be careful. If Voss has even an inkling of your trail, Tokyo will be swarming with his agents. You'll need to stay off the grid as much as possible."

Lian gave a short nod, disconnecting the call and slipping into her prep mode. Tokyo's labyrinthine underworld, teeming with rogue techies and off-grid data traffickers, would be the perfect cover—if she could avoid drawing attention.

The journey to Tokyo was uneventful, her route carefully planned to avoid digital checkpoints and surveillance hotspots. By the time she arrived, night had fallen, casting the city in a glow of neon signs and thrumming energy. The metropolis buzzed with life, a stark contrast to New Siberia's desolate tundra. She navigated through narrow backstreets and underground passages until she reached the entrance to a derelict subway station, where Kairo was rumored to operate.

As she descended into the dimly lit station, she sensed the unmistakable hum of live servers and encrypted networks lurking in the dark. Old subway cars, stripped of seats and filled with tech, lined the walls, their windows glowing faintly with the lights of monitors and equipment. She spotted a figure at the far end—a man hunched over a console, his fingers flying across the keyboard.

"Kairo?" she called out softly, keeping her voice low but firm.

He looked up, his gaze piercing, eyes lit by the glow of the monitor. "You must be Lian. Phantom sent word."

She approached, keeping her steps measured. "I have something that needs decrypting. A fragment of Project Requiem."

The mention of Requiem made him stiffen, his face hardening. He gestured for her to hand over the drive, his expression unreadable. "I'll see what I can do, but let's get one thing straight: Requiem's ghosts are dangerous. Those who dig too deep into its files don't usually live long enough to regret it."

"I'm aware," she replied, her tone steady. "I need the truth, Kairo. Whatever's left of it."

He nodded, inserting the drive into his system and running a decryption sequence. As the code unfurled on the screen, Lian watched, her heart pounding as each new line of text appeared. Kairo muttered under his breath, his fingers moving deftly as he bypassed encryption layers Phantom hadn't even touched.

After what felt like an eternity, Kairo leaned back, his face pale. "This isn't just data. It's a blueprint—a blueprint for global compliance, embedded with protocols designed to influence behavioral patterns, memories, and even emotional responses. Requiem wasn't just about erasure. It was about creating a new, compliant humanity."

He pointed to a section labeled *Phase IV—Emotional Manipulation and Cognitive Compliance Implementation*. The implications were chilling. This phase detailed the development of an algorithm that could alter memories, reshape personalities, and enforce loyalty to a singular global authority—VossCorp.

"What you're looking at is mind control on a scale the world has never seen," Kairo murmured, his voice tinged with awe and horror. "The Collapse was just the beginning. It was a trial run, a way to test these algorithms. Now VossCorp has the infrastructure, the tools to deploy this at full scale."

Lian felt the weight of his words sink in. Voss wasn't just rewriting history—he was rewriting humanity itself. The Collapse had been a test of society's resilience, a beta version of a world he sought to control completely.

"Can you access the rest of the files?" she asked, her voice barely a whisper.

Kairo nodded, his fingers moving swiftly as he unearthed additional fragments of Requiem's architecture. "There's a secondary hub located in New York. If you can reach it, there's a chance to access Requiem's central server and retrieve the unfiltered data before it goes live. But be warned, VossCorp is likely already watching every entry point to the network."

The gravity of her mission settled over her. Lian knew this was her last chance to expose the full scope of Voss's plans. If she could retrieve the data from New York, she'd have irrefutable proof of Requiem's design—proof that could turn the world against VossCorp.

Kairo handed her a new chip, his expression solemn. "This will get you into the New York hub's access points. I'll keep an eye on Voss's network from here, but once you're in, you're on your own."

She pocketed the chip, meeting his gaze with unwavering resolve. "Thank you, Kairo. For everything."

He gave her a faint nod, his eyes shadowed with worry. "Good luck, Lian. And if you succeed... don't forget those of us who helped you get there."

With one last glance at the lines of code still streaming across his monitor, she turned and left, slipping back into the night. The city lights cast sharp angles and deep shadows, making the streets seem like a living entity, holding its breath as she passed.

Her path was clear. The truth was closer than ever, and the final step awaited her in New York—a chance to uncover the darkest secrets VossCorp had kept hidden and, with it, a hope to rewrite the future.

6

Chapter 6: The Leak

The night air in New York was thick with the hum of distant traffic and the glow of city lights, casting everything in shades of electric blue and neon red. Lian Cheng moved through the shadows of the bustling megacity, blending into the crowd as she navigated her way to a hidden access point beneath the city. Phantom had arranged a safe route, but even he couldn't guarantee complete anonymity here; Voss-Corp had eyes everywhere, and the security in this part of the world was among the tightest she had encountered.

She adjusted her disguise—a nondescript jacket, hair tucked beneath a hood, and a pair of infrared-blocking glasses. New York was a fortress, its streets lined with surveillance drones, AI patrollers, and guards who looked more machine than human. She moved cautiously, her heart pounding, feeling each moment as a potential risk.

Her destination was a forgotten basement bunker once used as a makeshift headquarters by rogue hackers. Since the Collapse, however, it had been abandoned, its systems left to gather dust until now. Phantom had updated the bunker with encryption layers, making it the perfect place for her next move: releasing a fragment of Requiem's files into the underbelly of the net, exposing the conspiracy to a secretive circle of truth-seekers.

As she entered the bunker, the door clicked shut behind her, the silence settling thickly around her. She activated her equipment, fingers flying across the console as she prepared the files for a carefully orchestrated leak. It had to be subtle enough to avoid immediate detection by

VossCorp, yet significant enough to spark interest among those who understood the danger of Project Requiem.

The screen flared to life as her encryption software kicked in, the data flashing across her monitor, ready to be fragmented and scattered across a network of anonymous data forums and encrypted channels. She selected a fragment detailing *Phase II—Population Compliance Protocols*, a section exposing VossCorp's algorithmic manipulation of public sentiment and memory conditioning.

She hesitated, her fingers poised over the command. This fragment alone was powerful, but it barely scratched the surface of Requiem's full horrors. She knew that exposing it could lead to chaos—and that VossCorp would stop at nothing to erase both the information and her. But she couldn't ignore the weight of what she'd discovered; people needed to know.

With a quick breath, she pressed the key, initiating the upload. The file began to fracture, scattering across multiple encrypted forums and uploading in bursts that made it nearly impossible to track. The data would be visible only to those skilled enough to decipher it, the underground network of truth-seekers who lurked beyond the digital eye of VossCorp.

The first part of the leak was complete, but as she worked, she felt a prickling at the back of her neck—a sixth sense, honed from years on the run, warning her of unseen eyes. Just as the final files uploaded, her console flashed a red warning. A security breach. Somehow, her location had been compromised.

"Damn it," she muttered, scrambling to shut down the console and wipe her digital trace. Whoever was tracking her wasn't just guessing; they had pinpointed her precisely. Her screen flooded with static, a single message burning through the interference: **"You can't hide the truth forever."**

Her heart skipped. The message was followed by the unmistakable VossCorp insignia—a digital calling card from the corporation, a stark reminder that she was not alone. Her fingers flew over the keyboard, engaging her failsafe protocols, but the system lagged. Whoever was watching had a direct line into her network.

"Come on," she whispered, initiating a series of shutdown commands just as she heard the faint hum of drones outside.

She grabbed her backpack and bolted, barely making it to the exit as a group of heavily armed agents burst through the door. Lian ducked into the shadows, slipping into a narrow corridor that led to an underground maze of service tunnels. The agents spread out, their voices echoing as they issued commands, their footsteps close behind her.

She ran, every muscle in her body burning as she pushed through the dimly lit tunnels, her mind racing. The leak had been successful, but she had underestimated VossCorp's response time. They were faster, more relentless than she had anticipated. She would have to outwit them, evade their reach, if she was to survive long enough to release the rest of Requiem's files.

Her path twisted and turned, taking her deeper underground until she finally reached a maintenance room filled with old, forgotten machinery. She paused to catch her breath, adrenaline pulsing through her veins as she listened to the faint sounds of pursuit fading into the distance. Her pulse slowed, her mind clearing just enough to assess her next move.

Pulling out her portable console, she logged into an anonymous network, checking the status of her upload. Within hours, the fragment she had released would be circulating through dark-web forums and encrypted messaging channels. The implications would send shockwaves through underground networks, and she knew that curiosity would grow, sparking demands for more information. The truth about Project Requiem was now alive, rippling out like a shockwave, impossible to contain.

A soft ping alerted her to a new message. It was from Phantom, encrypted and marked urgent.

"Lian, they're tracking you. I just intercepted chatter on VossCorp's network—they know about the leak and have issued a level-one alert. Get out of there now."

She responded quickly, her fingers moving over the keys. "Where do I go? They're all over New York."

"Head south. There's a safehouse in the old subway tunnels. Stay low, and avoid any digital activity until you're clear. I'll monitor the network and divert them as best I can."

Lian didn't wait for more instructions. She stuffed her console back into her backpack and slipped out of the maintenance room, winding her way through the tunnels. Her heart pounded as she navigated the maze of corridors, each turn bringing her closer to escape—and farther from the safety of the city's familiar structure.

At last, she emerged into an abandoned section of the subway tunnels, her footsteps echoing in the darkened space. The air was thick and stale, the remnants of the old-world transit system forgotten in the wake of the Collapse. She moved swiftly, guided by Phantom's directions, her mind racing as she calculated her next move.

Reaching the designated safehouse, she ducked inside, sealing the door behind her. The room was small, lit only by the faint glow of emergency lights. It was sparse but functional—a cot, a few supplies, and a console that looked as though it hadn't been touched in years. She sank onto the cot, exhaustion crashing over her as she took a moment to breathe.

In the quiet, the weight of what she had done settled over her. The leak was the first step, a tiny crack in the fortress of lies VossCorp had constructed. But it was only the beginning. The fragment she had released was a tantalizing glimpse, enough to spark questions but far from the full truth.

Her thoughts were interrupted by another ping. Phantom's message appeared on her console, his tone urgent.

"Lian, things just got more complicated. Voss himself made a statement to his inner circle. He's launched a public misinformation campaign, spinning the leak as 'malicious propaganda' orchestrated by enemy states. They're going to bury the truth and frame it as a conspiracy."

Her fists clenched. Voss's tactics were ruthless; he was trying to drown the truth beneath layers of lies, casting doubt on the credibility of anyone who dared question him. This wasn't just a battle for survival—it was a war over the very nature of reality.

"Then we keep fighting," she replied, her resolve hardening. "There's more to Requiem, and I'll expose every last piece of it."

Phantom's response was immediate.

"There's no turning back now. But be careful. They won't stop until they have you. I'll keep tracking their movements, but stay hidden. And Lian... if you go down, make sure it's with the truth."

The message lingered on her screen, a reminder of the stakes she was up against. She knew that each step deeper into the web of Requiem brought her closer to the truth but also closer to VossCorp's reach. They would stop at nothing to silence her.

In the quiet darkness of the subway safehouse, Lian made a vow to herself. No matter how deep this conspiracy ran, no matter how ruthless Voss's reach, she would expose the full truth of Project Requiem. The world deserved to know, even if it cost her everything.

Chapter 7: Collateral Shadows

The first rays of dawn seeped into the tunnels, casting pale streaks of light that barely pierced the shadows surrounding Lian. She stood in the quiet of the underground safehouse, feeling the cold, damp air cling to her skin. The events of the previous night still weighed heavily on her—the leak, the narrow escape, and Voss's immediate retaliation. She knew that even in the brief moments of safety here, VossCorp was already working to eliminate any trace of her existence.

Pulling herself together, she checked her console for updates. As expected, the forums and encrypted channels were buzzing with activity, fragmented pieces of the Requiem data circulating among underground networks. The leak had taken root, and people were beginning to talk, questioning VossCorp's motives and drawing uncomfortable parallels to the Collapse. But the cost of that first strike had been steep; her safehouses across New York had already been compromised, their locations flagged by VossCorp surveillance teams.

A soft ping alerted her to a new message. It was from Phantom, his message clipped and urgent.

"Lian, they're tracking your known associates. Multiple units are canvassing New York and New Hong Kong, monitoring anyone you've contacted in the last few months. If you don't find a way to throw them off, they'll come for your network."

Her jaw tightened, her mind racing as she considered the implications. Voss wasn't just coming for her; he was targeting anyone who had crossed paths with her, anyone who could potentially hold even a sliver of information. And that included people who had no idea about her current mission.

She mentally cataloged her contacts—old colleagues from her days as a cybersecurity analyst, underground hackers, former clients she had helped during her early days in the shadows. Most had kept their distance since the Collapse, but a few had stayed in touch, providing her with critical intel and resources. They had trusted her, and now, unknowingly, they were at risk.

Her thoughts settled on one name in particular: **Mei Lin**, an old friend from her former life. Mei was a data analyst in New Hong Kong, someone who had worked with Lian to expose corporate corruption before the Collapse. They hadn't spoken directly in months, but Lian had used Mei's resources for Requiem's initial decryption without her knowing. If VossCorp was tracking her, Mei was a liability—someone they would easily find and exploit.

Cursing under her breath, Lian knew she couldn't leave her friend unprotected. She had to warn Mei, even if it meant putting herself further at risk.

Her fingers flew over the console, crafting an encrypted message.

"Mei, it's Lian. I don't have time to explain, but you're in danger. VossCorp is targeting my network, and they'll come for you. Drop everything, get off the grid, and don't contact anyone. Trust no one. I'll find you when it's safe."

She sent the message, adding layers of encryption to keep it hidden as long as possible. Once it was away, she turned her attention to the map on her console, plotting a path back to New Hong Kong. It would be risky, but she needed to ensure Mei could disappear before VossCorp's agents closed in.

Hours later, Lian arrived in New Hong Kong, slipping through the bustling city with practiced stealth. The streets buzzed with life, the hum of vendors and chatter punctuated by the distant thrum of drones overhead. Despite the urgency of her mission, she couldn't help but feel a strange sense of nostalgia, a reminder of her past life, before the Collapse, before the underworld had become her sanctuary.

Navigating through winding alleys, she made her way to Mei's apartment, a modest flat in a quiet district known for housing mid-level corporate employees. She paused, scanning the building for surveillance, feeling the tension in her muscles as she noted the faint glow of government-issued drones patrolling nearby. VossCorp's reach had already extended here.

She entered the building through a back entrance, her steps silent as she ascended the stairs. Reaching Mei's door, she tapped out a familiar code on the console outside, praying her friend was still here—and safe.

The door slid open, and Lian stepped inside, immediately greeted by Mei's startled expression. Mei was a slight woman with sharp features and keen, intelligent eyes. Those eyes widened as she took in Lian's worn appearance, understanding dawning on her face.

"Lian? What are you doing here?" Mei asked, her voice low but urgent.

"Mei, I need you to listen to me carefully," Lian replied, closing the door behind her. "You're in danger. VossCorp is targeting anyone connected to me. You have to disappear, now."

Mei's eyes flickered with a mix of fear and resolve. "This is about the Collapse, isn't it? You've found something... something they don't want anyone to know."

Lian nodded. "It's bigger than either of us could have imagined. Project Requiem—it wasn't just data erasure. VossCorp engineered it to control entire populations, to erase dissent by removing memories, even lives. They're coming for anyone who might have even the slightest connection to that truth."

Mei's face went pale. "And you... you're the one exposing this?"

"It doesn't matter. Right now, you need to get out," Lian said, her voice firm. "I'll help you disappear. But after this, you can't contact me, not until it's over."

Mei hesitated, a flash of anger breaking through her fear. "All these years, Lian. We fought together, and you never told me you were back in this."

"There wasn't time," Lian replied, regret lacing her tone. "If I could've kept you out of it, I would have. But now I need to know that you'll be safe."

Mei took a deep breath, the anger fading as she accepted the reality of the situation. "What do I need to do?"

Lian handed her a small device—an identity scrambler Phantom had equipped her with. "This will reset your data profile, making you invisible to their scanners. Go to the docks, find the black-market ferries. They'll take you to a safe zone outside the megacity."

Mei took the device, nodding. Her eyes met Lian's, filled with gratitude and a hint of sadness. "Stay safe, Lian. And finish this, whatever it takes."

"I will," Lian replied, giving her friend one last, brief embrace before slipping back into the shadows.

Returning to her own hiding place, Lian felt the weight of the decision settle on her. She had put Mei in danger simply by reaching out, and now Mei's survival was a gamble against VossCorp's relentless pursuit. But she couldn't let herself dwell on the cost; there was still work to be done, and more people at risk.

Her console beeped with another message from Phantom.

"Lian, VossCorp's agents are closing in. They've flagged three more of your contacts across New Hong Kong. You need to go dark."

She responded quickly. "Already moving. But we need to accelerate the next steps. The Requiem fragments are circulating, but without more data, people will dismiss it as rumors."

"Agreed," Phantom replied. "I've picked up chatter that Voss is preparing a counterattack—an info-dump to discredit the leak and bury the story under a mountain of lies. If he releases it, your data will be drowned out."

Lian's jaw clenched. Voss was a master at shaping public perception, and he knew exactly how to manipulate the truth. If she didn't act now, Requiem would be swept under a wave of propaganda, dismissed as conspiracy theories by a public eager to believe in the security VossCorp offered.

"Then we need the final piece of Requiem—the unfiltered data from the primary server," Lian replied. "If we can access it, we'll have everything. No one can deny the truth if they see the whole picture."

Phantom paused, then sent her a set of coordinates. "There's only one place that holds the master files for Requiem—an AI-protected server known as **The Nexus**. It's deep within VossCorp's main headquarters, embedded with sentries designed to erase any unauthorized presence. You'll have to go in-person; nothing can penetrate it remotely."

Her breath caught as she read the coordinates. Infiltrating VossCorp's headquarters was suicide, a fortress of technology and surveillance beyond anything she had faced. But there was no other option. The Nexus was the heart of Requiem, and without it, the world would never understand the full scale of Voss's plans.

She took a steadying breath, feeling a cold resolve settle over her. "I'm going for it. Meet me on the ground in New Hong Kong in twenty-four hours. I'll need everything you have."

"You know what you're up against," Phantom replied, a hint of apprehension in his voice. "This is all or nothing, Lian."

"I know," she said quietly. "And I won't let them erase us again."

As she disconnected, she allowed herself a brief moment to gather her thoughts, her mind turning to Mei and the others she had worked so hard to protect. This was it—the point of no return. The stakes had never been higher, but neither had her resolve.

Grabbing her pack, she made her way out of the safehouse, her gaze hard and unyielding as she prepared to take on the heart of VossCorp itself. In her hand, she held the last remnants of Requiem's fragmented data, and within her, the knowledge that, for better or worse, the final battle for truth was about to begin.

Chapter 8: Pursued by the Unseen

The rain fell in relentless sheets, blurring the lights of New Hong Kong into a haze of neon and shadow as Lian Cheng navigated through the winding back alleys of the city's lower districts. The streets were alive with the usual clamor, but tonight, a distinct unease settled over her. Phantom had warned her: this was the beginning of the endgame. VossCorp was tightening its grip, monitoring the city with a fleet of drones and patrolling agents, all primed to root her out.

Ahead of her loomed an abandoned subway entrance, leading down into the skeletal remains of a forgotten transport system beneath the city. It would take her deep into the veins of New Hong Kong, toward a secure location where Phantom waited with the final tools she would need to access VossCorp's impenetrable Nexus. She glanced over her shoulder, the faint whirring of drones barely audible over the rain. Her cover was fragile, every step a calculated risk.

As she descended into the shadows of the subway, the noises of the city faded, replaced by a cold, eerie silence. Flickering lights reflected off the damp, rusted walls, casting long, shifting shadows. She could feel the pulse of the city above her, every beat a reminder of the countdown ticking away in her mind. With each step closer to VossCorp's headquarters, she was narrowing the gap between her and an uncertain fate.

Reaching a hollowed-out service area deep within the tunnels, she paused, catching sight of Phantom waiting in the shadows. He looked up as she approached, his usual calm replaced by an intensity she hadn't seen before. The low light illuminated the sharp angles of his face, casting a shadow over his eyes, which glowed faintly from his visor.

"You made it," he said, his voice low and steady, though tinged with urgency.

"Barely," she replied, scanning the dark, hollowed walls around them. "They're everywhere. It's only a matter of time before they close in."

Phantom gave a grim nod. "That's why I've set up as many distractions as possible. There are decoy data bursts pinging across the city, enough to keep VossCorp's agents busy, but it won't hold them for long." He handed her a small, black device no larger than a coin. "This is your key to the Nexus. Once you're in, it'll disrupt the AI sentries long enough for you to access the files."

She took the device, feeling its weight in her palm. "And once I'm in, what then?"

"Once you're in the Nexus, look for the root file labeled *Core Directive*. It's where Requiem's unfiltered data is stored. If you can get it out, the entire structure of Requiem will be exposed. There will be no hiding for Voss or his empire."

Lian nodded, slipping the device into her pocket. "And if I can't get out?"

Phantom's jaw tightened. "If you're caught, VossCorp's AI will wipe your memories before you even understand what's happening. You'll be erased, Lian—not just from the grid but from existence."

A silence settled between them as she considered the magnitude of the mission ahead. Everything she had worked for, every risk she had taken, had led to this moment. Her fate, the truth, and the lives of everyone who had fallen to Voss's control depended on her success.

"I won't let them erase me," she replied, a fierce determination hardening her voice. "Or the truth."

Phantom gave a brief nod. "I'll be monitoring from here, tracking VossCorp's agents and rerouting them as best I can. But be careful—this part of the network is alive with counter-surveillance. If the sentries detect you, I may not be able to divert them fast enough."

With a final glance, Lian turned and headed deeper into the tunnels, leaving Phantom in the shadows. Each step echoed in the silent passage, the air thick with the weight of what lay ahead.

She reached the surface near VossCorp's towering headquarters, its sleek facade glinting in the dim light as if daring her to enter. From here, she could see the Nexus—a windowless, fortified structure attached to the main building, secured by layers of surveillance drones, biometric scanners, and sentry AI. It was designed to repel any intruder, especially one like her.

Timing her movements, Lian activated the small device Phantom had given her, feeling a faint hum as it created a distortion field around her. It was temporary, but it would give her just enough anonymity to slip past the outer surveillance without triggering immediate alarms. She moved swiftly, her eyes scanning every corner as she passed, alert for any sign of the AI sentries.

At the building's rear, she found a utility hatch—a narrow, seldom-used entry covered in security seals. She took a breath, knowing that once she breached this threshold, there would be no going back. She bypassed the seals with deft precision, slipping into the access shaft and descending into the labyrinthine passages beneath the Nexus.

The hallways were stark, bathed in sterile, artificial light that seemed to absorb sound. Every step was a risk, each corner a potential ambush. The security drones were silent, their scanning lights cutting across the floors and walls, but her device held firm, keeping her presence cloaked.

She reached a secure door marked *Core Access*, her pulse quickening. This was it—the heart of Requiem, where the most guarded truths of the Collapse were kept. She inserted the device, watching as it blinked, briefly disrupting the connection between the Nexus and its sentry AI. The door slid open with a quiet hiss, revealing a vast room lined with rows of servers, screens glowing with faint blue light.

Lian entered, her steps careful as she approached the central terminal. The console stood like a monolith in the room, its display flickering with streams of encrypted data. She connected her device to the console, watching as it began to unlock the files layer by layer. Her hands moved over the controls, each command peeling back years of lies and erasure.

As the decryption continued, lines of code revealed themselves, exposing phrases and project files that left her breathless.

"Requiem Phase IV: Behavioral Conditioning Algorithm."

"Cognitive Compliance Execution Protocol."

"Operation: Memory Purge."

She felt a chill as the implications sank in. This wasn't just about control or even surveillance. VossCorp had been systematically conditioning people, erasing memories and rewriting lives to fit a compliant, sanitized vision of society. Requiem wasn't just an experiment; it was a blueprint for a world under VossCorp's complete and total dominion.

At last, the file labeled *Core Directive* appeared on the screen. She accessed it, feeling the enormity of her discovery settle over her. This file held the root command for Requiem, the directive that allowed Voss to initiate and control every phase of the Collapse, every erased life, every altered memory. She copied the file to her device, her hands steady even as her heart raced. This was the proof she needed.

But as the data transfer neared completion, an alert blared through the room, red lights flashing as the AI sentries activated. She had been detected.

"Damn it," she whispered, pocketing the device as she glanced around for an escape route. The secure door she had entered through slammed shut, locking her in. The sentry AI had mobilized, blocking her only way out.

The room hummed, filling with the steady whir of drones as they descended from concealed compartments in the ceiling. Their scanning lights swept over her, sharp and unyielding. She activated the last of her countermeasures, hoping Phantom could disrupt the sentries long enough for her to escape.

Just then, her earpiece crackled to life. Phantom's voice came through, tense and strained. "Lian, I'm rerouting the drones, but they're adapting fast. I can buy you a few seconds, but you'll have to make a break for it."

"Understood," she replied, already calculating her next move.

She sprinted toward an emergency hatch on the far side of the room, dodging as drones attempted to cut off her path. The sentries adjusted, but she was faster, her body moving with practiced precision as she slid under one drone, barely avoiding its scanning light. Reaching the hatch, she forced it open, slipping into a narrow maintenance shaft as alarms blared behind her.

The shaft led her through a winding maze of corridors, the sounds of pursuit echoing through the walls. She could hear the mechanical hum of drones growing closer, their precision relentless. Phantom's voice came through again, his tone grim.

"Lian, they're sending a unit to intercept you at the next exit. You'll need to find another way out."

She gritted her teeth, turning down a side passage, her mind racing as she weighed her options. The drones were relentless, their movements perfectly synchronized to track her every turn. She activated the last of her scrambling tech, hoping it would be enough to throw them off.

Bursting through a final access door, she found herself in the sub-basement, a cavernous room filled with old, abandoned machinery. The sounds of pursuit faded as the drones recalibrated, trying to lock onto her new location. She moved quietly, searching for an exit, her senses heightened by the adrenaline coursing through her veins.

The silence was shattered by the low hum of another unit—a figure emerging from the shadows, his form obscured by a dark cloak, his visor glowing with an ominous light. He was unmistakably VossCorp, his presence radiating an aura of cold, calculated menace.

"You've gone far enough, Ms. Cheng," the man said, his voice calm, almost amused. "VossCorp's patience has limits, and you've exceeded them."

Lian's fists clenched, her mind racing as she sized him up. "The truth will come out. Requiem is exposed, and there's nothing you can do to stop it."

The man chuckled, stepping closer. "You underestimate VossCorp's reach. We don't erase just data—we erase legacies. You are nothing but a flicker, Ms. Cheng. And like all flickers, you will burn out."

In one swift motion, she activated the emergency device Phantom had given her, triggering a blinding flash that filled the room. The figure staggered back, momentarily disoriented, and she seized the moment, darting through an open passage and escaping into the darkness beyond.

As she ran, she felt the device in her pocket—a small drive containing the full, unfiltered truth of Project Requiem. She was bruised, exhausted, and marked for erasure, but the truth was hers. And for the first time, she felt the gravity of her mission truly resonate.

In the silence of the night, hidden within the shadows of New Hong Kong, Lian Cheng knew one thing: she was ready to bring the fight to Voss, no matter the cost.

Chapter 9: Phantom's Bargain

Lian Cheng moved like a ghost through the labyrinthine streets of New Hong Kong, clutching the drive containing the complete blueprint of Project Requiem. Her heart was a strange blend of exhilaration and dread. She had the truth—the irrefutable proof of VossCorp's global manipulation, its meticulously crafted plan to reshape humanity itself. But now that she held it, the question of how to reveal it loomed large. Voss's network was vast, and the information she carried was far too dangerous to trust to just anyone.

Her only chance lay in the Red Room, a covert, ever-shifting sanctuary of hackers and rogues who traded in classified data and secrets that could never see the light of day. But gaining access was no simple feat. Even with her credentials, she knew the Red Room's doors wouldn't open without someone on the inside vouching for her. And that left her with one choice: she needed Phantom.

Reaching a secluded corner of the city, she accessed a hidden terminal and sent an encrypted ping to Phantom's secure line. Moments later, his voice crackled through her earpiece, calm but with a subtle undercurrent of urgency.

"Lian, I thought I'd lost you back there."

She exhaled, tension briefly lifting at the sound of his voice. "Not yet. I have the files, Phantom. The whole picture. But there's no way I can release it without VossCorp catching wind. I need access to the Red Room."

A pause lingered before Phantom responded, his tone cautious. "The Red Room's no ordinary network, Lian. It's a refuge for some, a fortress for others, and once you enter, you're at the mercy of those inside. They'll want something in return for granting access."

"I figured as much," she replied, her voice steady. "What will it take?"

Phantom's silence stretched, and she could almost picture him weighing her words, considering the risks. Finally, he spoke, his voice clipped but resigned. "There's one person who can grant you immediate entry: a hacker known as *Cipher*. He has the trust of the Red Room's gatekeepers. If he vouches for you, they'll let you in. But Cipher isn't a fan of charity; he'll expect a trade, something significant."

"Do you know where to find him?" she asked, her voice tight with anticipation.

"Last I heard, he was working a circuit in Bangkok's data exchange. But be warned—Cipher's no ordinary hacker. He deals in secrets, lives for them, and he's as paranoid as they come. He'll want proof that you have something worth his time. Mentioning Requiem should be enough, but be prepared. He won't make this easy."

With Phantom's directions fresh in her mind, Lian set off, slipping through the city's underbelly and securing a route to Bangkok, one of the few places that rivaled New Hong Kong in both secrecy and digital complexity.

The journey to Bangkok was tense, each moment filled with an acute awareness of the danger around her. VossCorp's reach had extended across cities, and she knew she was never far from its gaze. By the time she arrived, dusk had settled, and the city came alive with a frenetic energy that pulsed through every alley and street corner.

The data exchange was hidden in plain sight, a seemingly innocuous tech repair shop wedged between neon-lit storefronts. Stepping inside, she was greeted by a wall of screens displaying strings of encrypted data and fragmented code. The shop's patrons moved in silence, their faces obscured, their devices buzzing with the pulse of clandestine operations.

In the corner, a man sat alone, his figure cloaked in shadow, a faint glow illuminating his hooded face. He was hunched over a console, fingers flying across the keyboard with rapid precision. Lian recognized him immediately from Phantom's description: Cipher.

She approached cautiously, her heart pounding as she fought to keep her expression neutral. Cipher glanced up as she neared, his eyes sharp and calculating, taking in her presence with a look that spoke of curiosity and caution.

"Cipher," she said quietly, her voice steady. "I'm here on behalf of Phantom. I need access to the Red Room."

Cipher raised an eyebrow, a hint of a smirk playing on his lips. "The Red Room, huh? Not many seek its doors without a good reason. And what exactly do you have that's worth my time?"

She met his gaze, her tone unwavering. "Project Requiem. The full directive. It's everything VossCorp doesn't want the world to know. I have it on me."

Cipher's face flickered with interest, his posture shifting as he leaned forward. "Requiem, you say? That's a name I haven't heard in a while. Voss's pet project... or so the rumors say. But rumors are cheap, and I don't deal in idle gossip."

"I'm not here to waste time," Lian replied, feeling the weight of the drive in her pocket. "I have the files, and they expose VossCorp's entire plan. But I need the Red Room's network to release them safely. In exchange, I'll give you exclusive access to parts of Requiem. Information that only I have."

Cipher considered her offer, his eyes narrowing as he weighed the risks. "You're asking for a lot. The Red Room isn't just a network; it's a sanctuary, a place where people go to disappear. And bringing in someone with VossCorp on their tail... that's risky."

"Cipher, this information could bring down VossCorp," she insisted. "It's worth more than just another secret. It's the truth about the Collapse, about the lives erased by Voss."

He leaned back, arms folded as he regarded her with an intense stare. "Fine," he said slowly. "But I want assurances. I get access to your data, no barriers, no restrictions. And if you survive, you owe me a favor. Red Room entry doesn't come cheap, and if you're still around once the dust settles, I expect you to remember that."

Lian gave a short nod, extending her hand. "Deal."

Cipher's grip was firm, his gaze unflinching. "Then follow me."

He led her through a series of hidden corridors, winding deeper into the data exchange until they reached a room lined with consoles and monitors. He keyed in a code, and a section of the wall slid back, revealing a hidden passage. They descended into a dimly lit corridor, the faint hum of machinery vibrating through the walls.

After what felt like an eternity, they reached a door marked only by a faint red light. Cipher placed his hand on a scanner, and the door slid open, revealing a vast chamber filled with rows of monitors and terminals, each manned by shadowed figures—hackers, data brokers, and digital experts from every corner of the underground network. This was the Red Room, the nerve center of secrets, a place where information flowed like blood in the veins of a hidden beast.

Cipher gestured to an empty console. "Plug in your drive. Let's see what you've got."

Lian approached the console, inserting the drive and watching as lines of code began to flash across the screen. Cipher's eyes widened as he scanned the data, his expression shifting from intrigue to astonishment.

"This... this is more than I expected," he muttered, his voice barely a whisper. "Phase IV, behavioral conditioning... cognitive compliance... Voss wasn't just erasing data; he was shaping entire populations."

He looked at her, a mixture of admiration and wariness in his gaze. "You weren't exaggerating. This is the real deal. But VossCorp will burn cities to the ground to prevent this from going public."

"That's why I need the Red Room's network," she replied, her voice firm. "I need a secure route to release this. I need allies who can protect the data and ensure it spreads faster than VossCorp can contain it."

Cipher nodded slowly. "We can help with that. But once this is out, there's no going back. VossCorp will come after everyone connected to this data. You'll be putting everyone here at risk."

Lian met his gaze, her voice steady. "I didn't come this far to turn back. I know the risks, and I'm prepared to face them."

Cipher turned to the assembled crowd, his voice carrying through the chamber. "We've got a choice here. This data... it's the truth about VossCorp, about the Collapse, about all the lives they erased. But releasing it means we're declaring war on one of the most powerful corporations in existence. If we do this, there's no turning back."

The silence was heavy, filled with the weight of a decision that would alter the course of their lives. One by one, heads began to nod, murmurs of agreement filling the room. They were hackers, truth-seekers, people who had spent their lives on the fringes, defying authority and hiding in the shadows. For them, this was more than just another job; it was a chance to expose the lies that had shaped their world.

Cipher turned back to Lian, his expression resolute. "Alright, we're in. The Red Room will back you. Let's bring VossCorp down."

With the network of the Red Room at her disposal, Lian prepared to release the data, setting up channels and routing points that would scatter Requiem's secrets across the globe. The truth would no longer be confined to the shadows. It would spread like wildfire, reaching the darkest corners and brightest screens, unstoppable, undeniable.

As she initiated the upload, she felt a surge of determination, a resolve that burned brighter than any fear. This was her chance—her moment to rewrite the world and expose the monstrous truth behind the Collapse.

In the Red Room's dim glow, surrounded by allies and secrets, Lian knew that the war had just begun.

Chapter 10: Unveiling the Conspiracy

The atmosphere in the Red Room was tense, every monitor and console buzzing with the incoming flow of data as Lian Cheng initiated the release of Project Requiem's files. Lines of encrypted code and classified directives danced across the screens, scattering VossCorp's secrets through the digital veins of underground networks, encrypted forums, and hidden data havens across the globe. Within moments, the truth was unleashed, setting off a chain reaction that would be impossible to contain.

As the data transfer continued, a hush fell over the room, the gravity of their actions settling over the assembled hackers and data brokers. Lian watched as Cipher worked tirelessly beside her, his fingers flying over the keyboard, rerouting the files through obscure paths that would keep the data safe from VossCorp's inevitable countermeasures.

One of the Red Room members, a wiry figure known as "Patch," turned to Lian, his face illuminated by the dim glow of his console. "These files... it's worse than we imagined. VossCorp wasn't just controlling data; they were controlling people, rewriting entire histories. They've wiped entire communities, reshaped the past."

Lian nodded, the weight of her discovery pressing down on her. "Project Requiem was never about maintaining order. It was about absolute control—erasing anything or anyone who dared stand in Voss's way. And the Collapse... it was just a test run, a way to see how far they could push the limits of their power."

Cipher glanced over, his expression grim. "Once this information reaches the surface, they'll come down hard. VossCorp has their agents embedded everywhere—from governments to corporations. They'll paint this as misinformation, as propaganda, and they'll hunt anyone connected to the leak."

Lian's gaze swept over the room, taking in the faces of those around her. They had chosen to stand beside her, to risk everything to bring the truth to light. And now, they were part of something much larger than a single hack or data leak. They were part of a movement—a resistance.

As the last of the files reached their destinations, a final message popped up on her screen: **"Upload Complete. Data Integrity Verified."** The truth of Requiem was now out there, unstoppable, a force unleashed on the world.

But even as she felt the relief of completion, the euphoria was short-lived. Alarms blared throughout the Red Room, the overhead lights flashing red as alerts poured across every screen. Lines of code filled the monitors, indicating a breach.

Cipher's face went pale. "They've found us."

Lian's pulse quickened as she glanced around, watching as members of the Red Room scrambled, inputting commands and activating emergency protocols. VossCorp's digital sentries had tracked the data trail to the Red Room, and they were closing in fast, their presence crawling through the network like a venomous cloud.

"We need to sever the main connection," Cipher shouted, his voice cutting through the chaos. "If they get a fix on our exact location, they'll send ground units!"

Lian didn't hesitate. She initiated a shutdown sequence, but even as she worked, she could feel the digital pressure of VossCorp's agents pressing down on them, probing for vulnerabilities, infiltrating layer by layer. They were relentless, their precision cold and calculated, like hunters closing in on wounded prey.

But even in the midst of the onslaught, Lian's mind raced with possibilities. If they could use VossCorp's own network to their advantage, they might be able to turn the tables. She leaned toward Cipher, her voice low but urgent. "Is there any way we can trace their path back? Use their connection to get into their own network?"

Cipher's eyes flashed with understanding. "A reverse trace... risky, but if we can break into their command line, we could plant our own data right into their headquarters. Expose them from the inside."

Without another word, the two of them initiated the reverse trace, their fingers moving in sync as they battled VossCorp's sentries, rerouting their code and breaking through firewalls. It was an all-out cyber war, each side fighting for control of the network. The Red Room's members fell silent, watching with a mix of fear and awe as Lian and Cipher engaged in a digital duel against one of the world's most powerful corporations.

After what felt like an eternity, a single line of text appeared on their screen: **Access Granted. Connection Secured.**

Cipher grinned, his eyes gleaming. "We're in. We have a direct line to VossCorp's command center."

Lian's heart raced as she entered VossCorp's core network, navigating through files and directories until she found what she was looking for: the hidden communication logs, the secret exchanges between Voss and his inner circle detailing the phases of Project Requiem, the approval of "memory recalibration" techniques, the ruthless erasure of individuals and histories.

But even as she scanned the files, her blood ran cold. Voss wasn't simply erasing memories—he was rewriting the world, crafting a new reality that served his empire's vision. It was mind control on a scale she had barely comprehended, a level of influence that went beyond physical borders and technological barriers.

"Lian," Cipher's voice broke through her thoughts, his tone urgent. "We need to get out of here. They're sending physical units. We're out of time."

She forced herself to focus, copying the last of the critical files and embedding a digital bomb—a failsafe that would release the entire collection of files into VossCorp's own intranet, making the data impossible to contain. Once activated, VossCorp's own systems would betray them, broadcasting their secrets across their entire infrastructure.

They disconnected just as the Red Room began to power down, the hackers executing their emergency evacuation protocols. Lian grabbed her drive, her heart pounding as she followed Cipher and the others out of the chamber, navigating through the labyrinthine tunnels beneath the city.

The echoes of footsteps and the faint hum of drones grew louder as they approached the surface. VossCorp's ground units were mobilizing, their presence like a shadow spreading over the city, poised to strike. Cipher led them through a series of concealed exits, winding through back alleys and hidden passages until they emerged in the dim light of a narrow, secluded street.

They had barely taken a breath before a drone whirred overhead, its scanner light sweeping the alley. Lian pressed against the wall, her heart racing as the beam passed inches from her face. But the drone continued on, missing them by a fraction of a second.

Cipher looked over, his face pale but resolute. "We have to keep moving. They'll have every access point covered. But there's a safehouse on the outskirts—we can regroup there."

They moved swiftly, slipping through the city's darkened alleys, evading patrols, their every sense heightened by the knowledge that they were being hunted. By the time they reached the safehouse, they were exhausted, their nerves frayed, but they were alive—and they had the proof.

Inside the safehouse, the members of the Red Room gathered around a single console, the tension thick as they monitored the fallout of the release. Cipher typed a few commands, and a series of encrypted feeds appeared on the screen. News outlets, anonymous forums, even corporate channels were buzzing with the leaked data. The truth was spreading like wildfire.

Lian's gaze was fixed on the screen, her heart pounding as she watched the impact unfold. She could see the disbelief, the shock, the outrage as people began to understand the depth of VossCorp's deception. Project Requiem's secrets were out, and the world was waking up to the monstrous reality behind the Collapse.

Phantom's voice crackled over the line, his tone charged with excitement. "You did it, Lian. They can't bury this now. The truth is out."

But even as the realization sank in, she knew this was only the beginning. VossCorp wouldn't go down without a fight, and the release of Requiem's data would only fuel their determination to silence her and everyone involved.

Cipher turned to her, his eyes serious. "They'll retaliate. VossCorp will throw everything they have at us. But we're not alone now. The Red Room stands with you, and there are others out there—people who've seen the truth, who won't sit quietly anymore."

Lian met his gaze, a fierce determination settling over her. "Then let them come. Voss built his empire on lies, but now the world knows. We'll keep fighting until there's nothing left for him to hide behind."

In the flickering light of the console, surrounded by allies and the burning embers of resistance, Lian felt the full weight of her mission settle over her. The truth had been set free, and there was no turning back. She had ignited a revolution, a war for memory, for truth, for freedom from the chains of digital erasure.

As the dawn broke over New Hong Kong, casting a pale light over the city, Lian knew that the battle had only just begun.

Chapter 11: Seeds of Revolution

The streets of New Hong Kong were teeming with an undercurrent of unrest as the truth of Project Requiem spread. Lian Cheng moved through the throngs of people, her hood pulled low, concealing her face as she watched the city awaken to the dark reality of VossCorp's control. Screens mounted on towering billboards flashed with distorted images, government officials denouncing the data leaks as a "misinformation campaign designed to destabilize public trust." But it was too late. Whispers filled the alleys, murmurs of outrage, of betrayal—people who had once placed their faith in the stability offered by VossCorp now felt the weight of the deception.

In the days following the release, anonymous groups sprung up across the network, forming underground channels to share and analyze the Requiem files. Citizens gathered in encrypted forums, discussing the extent of VossCorp's reach, the lives erased, the histories rewritten. Lian saw in these groups the seeds of something powerful—something that VossCorp would never be able to fully control.

Her destination was a secluded safehouse on the outskirts of New Hong Kong, where Phantom and Cipher waited, monitoring the growing resistance. As she slipped inside, Cipher looked up, his face lined with exhaustion but alight with a glimmer of hope.

"It's happening, Lian," he said, gesturing to the screens. "Forums, message boards, encrypted calls... people are demanding answers. The leak is spreading through every major network, even breaching corporate sites. We've finally got them on the defensive."

Lian nodded, her gaze scanning the screens filled with data feeds and message threads. "But it won't last. VossCorp will counter this with force if they have to. They'll do whatever it takes to keep the truth buried."

Phantom turned from his console, his expression grim but resolved. "We've already seen the first signs of retaliation. VossCorp's agents are making arrests, targeting anyone who's openly connected to the leak. They're tightening surveillance in every major city. But people aren't backing down. They're sharing the files faster than VossCorp can erase them."

Lian felt a surge of pride and fear for those brave enough to stand against VossCorp's regime. She had sparked a movement, but with that came a responsibility to see it through, to ensure that the people who risked everything for the truth wouldn't be silenced.

Cipher leaned forward, his fingers tapping out commands as he pulled up a new feed. "There's something else you should see," he said, his voice low. "A message from someone claiming to have insider knowledge on VossCorp's next move. It's encrypted and routed through a dozen anonymous servers, but it seems legit."

He handed her a device, the screen flickering as the message decrypted.

"VossCorp has activated Operation Compliance. They're deploying control protocols across global networks to silence resistance and monitor any remaining supporters. They'll use cognitive compliance algorithms to pacify dissent. Act fast, or all momentum will be lost."

Lian's heart sank as she read the message. Operation Compliance was more than just damage control; it was an all-out digital assault designed to suppress any trace of Requiem's truth. VossCorp was preparing to launch a new phase of control, one that would clamp down on not just information but on thoughts, emotions, and memories—a complete rewrite of reality for anyone under its digital gaze.

She looked up, her gaze meeting Phantom's. "If they deploy these protocols, the world will be forced into compliance. They'll erase this movement, rewrite people's minds to accept their narrative."

Phantom's jaw tightened, his fingers flying over his console as he scanned for signs of the activation sequence. "We need to disrupt it before they can launch. If we can overload their command center or intercept their core signal, we might be able to stop the deployment."

Cipher frowned, studying the lines of code scrolling across the screen. "Their control center is heavily fortified, guarded by their most advanced AI sentries. Breaking through will be nearly impossible."

"Then we'll have to find another way in," Lian said, her mind racing. "If we can get someone on the inside, someone close enough to manually disable the system from within, it might buy us the time we need to expose the full extent of Operation Compliance."

A tense silence settled over the room as they weighed the enormity of the task. But Lian's resolve only grew stronger. She had come this far, risked everything, and now she was prepared to go all the way. She glanced at Cipher and Phantom, her voice steady.

"I'll go in. VossCorp doesn't know I have Requiem's files. They'll be looking for resistance groups, not one rogue operator. If I can reach the control center, I'll upload a failsafe—a program that will loop the system's commands, forcing their sentries to overwrite themselves. It'll be risky, but it's our best shot."

Phantom's eyes narrowed, his face a mask of determination. "If you're going in, you'll need backup. I can create a decoy operation, a simulated attack on VossCorp's outer network to draw their attention away from the control center."

Cipher added, "I can provide you with a new set of encryption layers and a cloaking device to keep you hidden from their digital scanners. Once you're inside, I'll work to keep their system scrambled."

They worked through the night, strategizing, programming, refining every detail of the plan. By dawn, they had a clear course of action—one that would either dismantle VossCorp's latest attempt to tighten its grip on humanity or seal their fates forever.

The next night, Lian made her way to the outskirts of VossCorp's command center, the cloaking device keeping her hidden from the sentries patrolling the perimeter. The building loomed in the distance, a fortress of steel and glass, its every angle and line radiating an air of untouchable power.

She navigated the outer layers of security, moving through concealed routes mapped out by Phantom and Cipher, her heart racing as she slipped past checkpoints and scanning beams. Every step brought her closer to the control center, each turn a reminder of the fragility of her mission.

As she reached the core entrance, a wave of unease washed over her. Her device hummed softly, its sensors flashing a warning. Someone—or something—was monitoring the area, an AI sentry lurking just beyond her sight. She froze, waiting for a gap in its pattern, and slipped through, her body tense as she moved toward the mainframe chamber.

Inside, the room was bathed in a sterile blue light, rows of servers stretching out like digital sentinels. The central command console stood alone, a monolithic structure housing VossCorp's most sensitive operations. Lian moved swiftly, plugging her device into the terminal and initiating the failsafe program. Lines of code flashed across the screen as the program uploaded, its commands looping through the system, creating a digital feedback that would disrupt Operation Compliance.

But just as the program neared completion, an alert blared through the room, red lights flashing as an AI presence flooded the network. VossCorp's command AI had detected her intrusion.

"Unauthorized access detected," the system's voice droned, cold and impersonal. "Initiating lockdown sequence."

Panic threatened to grip her, but she forced herself to stay calm, her fingers flying over the controls as she manually rerouted the program, accelerating the upload. She could hear the faint hum of sentry drones closing in, their mechanical footsteps echoing down the hallway.

The program hit 90 percent, 91, 92... each second stretching into an eternity.

Just as the upload reached 99 percent, a squad of drones burst into the room, their scanners locking onto her. She activated the cloaking device, ducking out of their line of sight, her pulse pounding as the final command sequence loaded.

The screen flashed, confirming the upload. The failsafe was active, embedding itself into VossCorp's network, scrambling the cognitive compliance protocols just as they were set to deploy. The sentries froze, their movements stalling as the system looped, forcing their algorithms to overwrite themselves, a temporary chaos infiltrating Voss's carefully orchestrated empire.

In that moment, she heard Phantom's voice crackle over her earpiece, the relief evident in his tone. "Lian, you did it. Operation Compliance is offline. VossCorp's network is in disarray. The people are mobilizing—they're finally seeing VossCorp for what it is."

She allowed herself a breath, the weight of the moment sinking in. The failsafe had worked, but her mission wasn't over. As long as VossCorp remained intact, the threat would never be fully gone. But now, the resistance had a chance. A real chance.

Cipher's voice cut through the channel. "Lian, get out of there now. Reinforcements are closing in."

She took one last look at the terminal, her resolve hardening. The seeds of revolution had been planted, and the people would not be silenced again.

As she slipped out of the command center, evading VossCorp's forces, she felt a new purpose burning within her. This wasn't just her fight anymore. The world was awake, the people were rising, and VossCorp's reign of control was crumbling.

In the shadows of New Hong Kong, Lian Cheng vanished into the night, knowing that the war for truth had only just begun.

Chapter 12: Voss Strikes Back

In the weeks following the disruption of Operation Compliance, the world had transformed. Newsfeeds and forums buzzed with talk of the Requiem files, people on the streets openly questioned VossCorp's intentions, and protests flared across major cities. Citizens organized resistance groups, mobilizing digital networks to spread their message and counter VossCorp's propaganda machine. The seeds of revolution had taken root, and Lian Cheng could see the power of the truth spreading like wildfire.

But she knew this victory would come at a cost. Voss was not a man to back down, and his corporation would never relent in their pursuit to reclaim control.

The first sign of Voss's counterattack came in New Hong Kong, where a sudden power outage swept through the city, followed by a blackout of digital communications. People were left in darkness, their devices and screens flickering with static, as if Voss himself were reminding them of his reach.

Lian crouched in her safehouse, the room dimly lit by a single emergency light. Phantom's voice crackled through her earpiece, his tone laced with urgency.

"Lian, we're getting reports from all over. VossCorp's launched a coordinated assault on key data centers and communication hubs. They're erasing data trails, scrambling signals, and isolating resistance groups."

"Can we stop them?" she asked, knowing the scope of VossCorp's resources.

"We're doing everything we can, but Voss has activated a secondary protocol—a purge designed to identify and eliminate anyone connected to Requiem. They're systematically hunting down leaders in the resistance, tracking any remaining communication streams. They're calling it *Operation Clean Slate*."

The weight of Phantom's words settled over her, her mind racing. Operation Clean Slate was a ruthless, zero-tolerance campaign designed to silence dissenters by any means necessary. VossCorp's strategy was clear: to terrorize, isolate, and ultimately extinguish the resistance.

Cipher's voice chimed in, his usual confidence tinged with frustration. "They've already taken down two of our largest hubs in New Moscow and New Cairo. They're moving fast, shutting down entire networks, and they have AI watchdogs monitoring every movement. If we don't disrupt this purge soon, Voss will lock down every major resistance channel."

Lian clenched her fists, determination burning within her. "We need a way to outmaneuver them. If Voss is using Clean Slate to track us, we need to go where they can't follow—deeper into the system, into VossCorp's own blind spots."

Phantom was quiet for a moment, then spoke, his tone contemplative. "There's one place VossCorp rarely monitors, a dead zone buried deep within their oldest archives. It's called the *Obsidian Vault*. The vault holds classified files and forgotten fragments from before the Collapse. If we can reach it, we might find a way to neutralize Clean Slate from within VossCorp's own infrastructure."

Cipher's voice was skeptical. "You're talking about infiltrating VossCorp's most secure server, an area even their highest executives can barely access. You're asking for a suicide mission."

Lian's voice was steady. "We've come this far. If we can cripple Clean Slate, it will give the resistance time to organize, to mobilize before VossCorp reclaims control. We have to try."

Phantom responded with a resolute nod. "I'll prepare the tools you'll need, but getting into the Obsidian Vault will require bypassing layers of security, each one more lethal than the last. Voss has likely upgraded every firewall and security protocol after Operation Compliance."

Lian took a breath, steadying herself. "Tell me what I need to do."

The journey into VossCorp's headquarters was like descending into a labyrinth of glass and steel, each step taking her deeper into the heart of a corporation that saw itself as a god. The Obsidian Vault lay buried beneath layers of security and deception, guarded by AI sentries and hidden from the public eye, a secret even many within VossCorp knew nothing about.

Dressed in a dark, hooded suit equipped with Phantom's cloaking tech and Cipher's advanced encryption layers, Lian moved through the lower levels of VossCorp, evading cameras and biometric scanners. Every corner of the building radiated cold efficiency, designed with perfect symmetry and inhuman precision.

She passed through corridor after corridor, each one more desolate than the last, until she reached a nondescript door marked only with a faint code etched into the wall. This was the entrance to the Obsidian Vault, hidden in plain sight, a place too secret to be overtly protected.

With a deep breath, she activated Cipher's encryption device, bypassing the door's security with a soft click. She entered, feeling a chill as she stepped into the Vault. The room was cold, a sterile chamber lined with servers glowing a deep, pulsating blue. At its center stood a single console, its screen flickering with lines of data from before the Collapse, records of government alliances, experiments, and forgotten technological advancements that VossCorp had absorbed in its rise to dominance.

Lian approached the console, feeling the weight of history embedded in its circuits. She connected Phantom's device, watching as lines of code scrolled across the screen, giving her access to the deepest layers of VossCorp's network. Each layer revealed pieces of Operation Clean Slate, detailing the locations of resistance hubs, the identities of leaders, and protocols for systematic "neutralization."

As she sifted through the files, she found a core command buried within Clean Slate's algorithm—a failsafe that, if triggered, could disrupt the entire operation. Her fingers moved swiftly, isolating the command and preparing it for execution. But as she initiated the override, the console froze, an error message flashing across the screen.

The lights dimmed, and a voice filled the room—a voice cold, calculated, and painfully familiar.

"Lian Cheng. You've come far. Farther than I anticipated."

She turned, her heart pounding as Elias Voss himself stepped out of the shadows. He was tall, impeccably dressed, his face bearing the faintest trace of a smirk as he regarded her with an unsettling calm.

"Do you really believe you can dismantle an empire with a few data leaks and fragmented files?" he asked, his voice smooth, almost amused.

Lian forced herself to meet his gaze, her voice steady. "The truth is out, Voss. People are waking up. They won't go back to sleep."

Voss tilted his head, his expression unreadable. "The truth, Ms. Cheng, is a malleable thing. It bends, shifts, until it becomes whatever I desire. You see, I control the networks, the data, the memories. I decide what people believe, what they remember, and what they forget."

Lian's hands tightened into fists. "You can't erase this. The people won't let you."

Voss's eyes gleamed with a chilling certainty. "People crave stability, Ms. Cheng. They want safety, order. And when they see the chaos your so-called 'truth' brings, they'll beg for me to restore it. They'll abandon this 'resistance' of yours and return to my version of reality—because it is simpler, safer."

He stepped closer, his gaze piercing. "You have two choices, Ms. Cheng. Surrender, and I might consider preserving some semblance of your identity. Or refuse, and I'll erase you from history, just as I have countless others. I'll erase every ally you've made, every contact, every whisper of your existence. You will become nothing."

She stared at him, feeling the weight of his threat, the vast power he wielded, the chilling certainty in his eyes. But as she looked at him, she felt a surge of defiance, a spark of resistance that burned hotter than any fear.

"Erase me if you can, Voss. But you'll never erase the truth."

With a swift motion, she activated Phantom's device, embedding the failsafe into the command line. Voss's face darkened as he realized what she was doing, his calm facade breaking for a split second.

"You fool!" he hissed, lunging for the console. But it was too late—the failsafe triggered, sending a pulse through VossCorp's network, disrupting Clean Slate's algorithms and spreading a cascading virus through the corporation's central infrastructure.

The lights flickered, the servers humming erratically as the failsafe rewrote the protocols, blocking Clean Slate's commands and restoring the encrypted communication lines that VossCorp had severed. The resistance networks blinked back to life, their channels flooding with messages of triumph, of hope, of victory.

Voss staggered back, his face twisted in fury, but his control over the situation was slipping, the power he wielded beginning to crumble.

"You think this will stop me?" he spat, his voice laced with venom. "I am VossCorp. I am the architect of this world. And I will reshape it in my image, no matter how many times I have to rebuild it."

Lian met his gaze, her voice unyielding. "You've built an empire on lies, Voss. But people know the truth now. They won't go back."

The room trembled, the servers sparking as the failsafe continued its work, embedding itself deeper into VossCorp's network, corrupting Clean Slate and rendering it inert. Lian knew her time was running out, but she felt a fierce satisfaction, a sense of purpose that outweighed any fear.

As alarms blared throughout the facility, she turned and ran, slipping through the corridors as Voss's empire began to fracture around her. The weight of his words lingered, but the strength of her conviction pushed her forward. She had planted a seed of revolution, and Voss's reach was not infinite. The people now held a power that even he couldn't erase.

And as she vanished into the night, the fires of resistance burned brighter than ever, a testament to a world that had finally woken up.

Chapter 13: The Digital Blackout

The streets of New Hong Kong lay cloaked in a surreal silence as a sudden digital blackout descended over the city. Lian Cheng moved swiftly through the shadows, her heart pounding as she navigated the darkened alleys. The pulse of neon signs and holographic ads had vanished, leaving only an eerie, stifling stillness. Above, the high-rise towers of the wealthy stood as dark monoliths against the cloudy sky, their usual glow extinguished.

She knew this was VossCorp's doing. After the sabotage of Operation Clean Slate and the disruption within the Obsidian Vault, Voss had unleashed his most desperate move yet: a citywide blackout, severing the digital lifelines that New Hong Kong relied on. Communications were cut, security drones grounded, and data centers locked down in an attempt to smother the resistance by any means necessary.

But the blackout was also a double-edged sword. While it hampered the resistance, it also hindered VossCorp's surveillance network, disrupting their ability to monitor and control the populace. In this silence, the resistance had a rare opportunity—a window to regroup, to strategize, and, with luck, to deliver the final blow.

Lian reached an abandoned metro station where members of the resistance had gathered, their faces barely visible in the dim light of emergency torches. Phantom and Cipher were already there, their expressions grim as they scanned the group, readying them for what lay ahead.

"Voss is desperate," Phantom said, his voice low but steady. "This blackout is his last-ditch effort to regain control. He's shut down the entire network, hoping to isolate us and crush any remaining dissent. But he's made a mistake. By cutting himself off, he's blind to what's happening down here."

Cipher nodded, pulling up a manual map on a small, offline device. "The blackout has cut power to all major facilities, including VossCorp's primary data servers. If we can reach their central energy grid and disable it completely, we could shut down their backup systems and disable any remaining servers. VossCorp's command center will go dark, and with it, Voss's hold on New Hong Kong."

Lian's mind raced, absorbing the plan. "But without power, how will we coordinate with the rest of the resistance?"

Cipher flashed a small, confident smile. "We'll be using an analog signal—a manual relay through encrypted radios we've distributed among resistance cells across the city. It's a primitive system, but it's undetectable by VossCorp's digital infrastructure. They won't see it coming."

The group quickly divided into teams, each tasked with reaching a critical point in VossCorp's energy grid. Lian's team would be responsible for infiltrating the primary control hub—a heavily fortified building at the heart of the city's energy network. It was one of the few places still operating on limited backup power, its systems designed to protect against exactly the kind of assault they were about to mount.

As the teams moved out, Lian found herself alongside a few familiar faces: Cipher, his gaze focused and determined; Patch, the wiry hacker who had been a part of the Red Room's earlier operation; and a handful of others whose resolve seemed unbreakable, despite the dangers ahead.

They moved through the streets, sticking to the shadows, every sound amplified by the surrounding silence. VossCorp's agents patrolled in small units, relying on handheld lights to guide their way. The blackout had leveled the playing field, giving the resistance a unique advantage.

As they reached the perimeter of the energy grid, Lian signaled for the team to pause. The control hub loomed before them, a stark, windowless structure wrapped in steel and concrete, its surface reflecting the dim glow of emergency lights. They would have to move quickly and quietly to avoid detection.

Cipher glanced at Lian, his expression serious. "We'll need to bypass the security manually. Once we're inside, we'll split up—Patch and I will handle the mainframe, while you secure the backup generators. We'll have less than ten minutes before their sentries realize something's wrong."

Lian nodded, her mind already mapping out her path. They moved forward, evading the patrolling guards and slipping through a side entrance that Cipher had managed to disable. Inside, the building was cold and silent, the hum of backup power the only sound as they navigated the narrow corridors.

The team split, with Cipher and Patch heading toward the mainframe while Lian made her way to the backup generator room. The air was thick with tension, every shadow a potential threat, every echo a reminder of the urgency of their mission.

Reaching the generator room, Lian studied the rows of machines, each one a complex array of circuits and conduits that kept VossCorp's command center operational. She moved swiftly, connecting Phantom's device to the main control panel, initiating a program that would shut down each generator in sequence, ensuring a total blackout within the command center itself.

As she worked, her earpiece crackled to life. It was Cipher, his voice tense. "Lian, we're in position. Mainframe access is secured. Initiate the shutdown on your mark."

Lian took a deep breath, her fingers hovering over the control panel. She knew that this would leave VossCorp defenseless, vulnerable to the resistance. It was the moment they had all been fighting for, a chance to sever the empire's lifeblood and cripple its ability to control the city.

"Mark," she said, her voice steady.

She triggered the shutdown sequence, watching as the lights in the generator room flickered and dimmed, each machine powering down in succession. The hum of the backup power faded, replaced by an eerie silence that seemed to settle over the entire building.

But just as the last generator powered down, a blaring alarm cut through the silence, red lights flashing as the system registered the breach. Lian's heart raced as she heard the unmistakable sound of drones activating nearby. VossCorp's security protocol had detected the blackout, and the command center was going into lockdown.

Cipher's voice came through her earpiece, urgent and strained. "We're exposed. The sentries are on us. We'll have to fight our way out."

Lian didn't hesitate. She activated a scramble device, creating a temporary cloaking field around her as she slipped out of the generator room, her every sense heightened as she navigated the darkened corridors. She could hear the whir of drones approaching, their scanning lights casting erratic beams through the shadows.

As she moved through the maze-like hallways, she saw Cipher and Patch up ahead, ducking into cover as a squad of drones rounded the corner. They exchanged quick nods, their silent communication a testament to the trust they had built over these past weeks.

With practiced precision, they moved as a unit, using every ounce of stealth and agility to evade the drones. But as they neared the exit, a group of guards blocked their path, weapons raised, their eyes cold and unyielding.

One of the guards stepped forward, his voice dripping with contempt. "Did you really think you could outmaneuver VossCorp? The city belongs to us. You're just a pest, a nuisance we'll soon forget."

Lian's gaze hardened, her grip on her weapon tightening. "Maybe you can control the city," she replied, her voice low and resolute, "but you'll never control the people."

With a swift motion, she fired, her shot hitting the guard squarely, sending the others into a flurry of chaos. Cipher and Patch joined in, the corridor erupting in a cacophony of gunfire and flashing lights as they fought their way through the guards.

The battle was fierce, each second stretching into a tense struggle for survival. But at last, they broke through, slipping out of the building and disappearing into the darkness beyond.

As they regrouped outside, Lian could feel the surge of victory tempered by the knowledge that VossCorp would not back down easily. But as she looked at her companions, their faces lined with exhaustion but alight with determination, she knew that they had struck a critical blow. The blackout had severed VossCorp's control over New Hong Kong, disrupting their infrastructure and buying the resistance time to mobilize.

Phantom's voice came through, his tone filled with relief. "We've done it, Lian. VossCorp is in disarray, and the people are flooding the streets. The blackout may have been Voss's move, but we turned it against him."

Lian allowed herself a brief, satisfied smile. The city, once shrouded in fear, was now alive with resistance. The people were rising, their voices echoing through the streets, their defiance a powerful testament to the strength of truth.

In the dim light of dawn, Lian and her companions vanished into the city, knowing that the blackout had marked a turning point in their war for freedom. Voss's empire was beginning to crumble, and the world was finally waking up.

Chapter 14: Into the Heart of Control

The city hummed with the energy of resistance as dawn broke over New Hong Kong. Crowds gathered in hushed groups, sharing stories, encrypted data, and fragments of the Requiem files that VossCorp had failed to fully contain. Lian Cheng moved quietly through the city's narrow alleys, her thoughts focused on the mission ahead: to enter VossCorp's central command—the heart of control—and dismantle the very system that kept the corporation's empire in power.

Phantom's voice crackled through her earpiece as she made her way toward the towering monolith that housed VossCorp's mainframe. "Lian, the resistance is holding steady, but Voss is retaliating faster than expected. The backup systems are coming online across New Hong Kong, and surveillance is doubling by the hour. If we're going to hit him where it hurts, it has to be now."

"Understood," Lian replied, her voice steady. "How's the support on the ground?"

"People are rallying in every district," he said. "They're tired of the lies, tired of the erasures. But they're waiting for a signal. Something concrete, a win that proves VossCorp isn't invincible."

Lian understood. The blackout had given the resistance momentum, but a victory within VossCorp's own headquarters would be the blow that solidified the movement's strength. It would be a symbol of defiance, of hope.

Her gaze lifted to the towering structure before her, the sleek facade of VossCorp's main command building rising against the morning sky. The building was a fortress, its entrances guarded by sentries and its perimeter covered by multiple layers of security drones. At the top, in a highly secure, isolated server room, lay the mainframe—the "Heart of Control," as it was known within VossCorp. It was here that the central data on every citizen, every transaction, and every piece of manipulated history was stored and managed. If she could reach it, she could dismantle Voss's surveillance network from within.

Cipher's voice joined the conversation. "Lian, the Heart of Control is heavily fortified, even more so than the Obsidian Vault. Voss has equipped the mainframe with sentient AI guardians that respond to any unauthorized presence. Getting in is a near-impossible task."

"Then let's make it possible," Lian replied, her voice unflinching. "I need a direct route to the Heart. Something that keeps me off the radar as long as possible."

Cipher hesitated, but after a moment, a new route appeared on her display, highlighting an entrance through the building's ventilation system—a narrow, winding path that would bypass most of the lower-level security. "This route will take you close, but there's no avoiding the final layer of protection. You'll be on your own once you reach the mainframe."

"Thanks, Cipher. I'll take it from there," she said, steadying herself for the task ahead.

The path through the building's ventilation system was cramped and dark, the air thick with the smell of recycled metal and stale dust. Lian moved silently, her every muscle tense as she navigated the winding ducts, her mind racing as she mentally prepared for the final showdown. She knew that once she entered the Heart of Control, she would be in the belly of Voss's empire, surrounded by his most advanced security and AI defenses.

When she reached the end of the vent, she pried open the grate, dropping soundlessly into a cold, sterile hallway illuminated by a faint blue glow. She was on the seventy-fifth floor now, just one level below the mainframe. Her cloaking device was active, masking her presence from the cameras, but she knew it would only buy her a limited amount of time.

The final stairwell leading to the Heart of Control was guarded by two AI sentries—metallic figures with sleek frames and glowing visors that pulsed with a red light as they scanned the area. She waited, studying their movements, noting the brief pause in their patrol route that would allow her to slip past. With one last breath, she moved swiftly, darting forward and slipping into the stairwell just as the sentries rounded the corner.

At the top of the stairs was a massive steel door marked with a digital lock. She pulled out Cipher's last tool—a signal disruptor designed to bypass biometric locks and override high-security access codes. The disruptor hummed, sending a ripple of static through the air as it worked, and with a quiet beep, the lock disengaged.

The door slid open, revealing a vast room bathed in the cool glow of screens and servers. At the center stood the Heart of Control itself—a towering, cylindrical mainframe, its core pulsing with a steady rhythm that seemed to match the heartbeat of the building. Data scrolled across the screens lining the walls, a cascade of information that represented the very essence of VossCorp's power.

Lian moved toward the mainframe, her fingers trembling slightly as she connected her device to the central console. She could feel the weight of the moment, the enormity of the task at hand. The console flashed to life, displaying a complex interface, its commands hidden behind layers of encryption.

Phantom's voice came through her earpiece, soft but resolute. "You're in, Lian. You have access to the Heart of Control. It's up to you now."

She activated the decryption program, watching as lines of code unraveled, exposing the layers of data and algorithms that formed the core of VossCorp's surveillance network. Here, she could see the files that dictated memory recalibrations, behavioral conditioning protocols, and the tracking records of thousands—possibly millions—of individuals. Every manipulated memory, every erased life, was encoded within this machine.

As the decryption continued, a command line appeared on the screen: **"Initiate Full System Override."**

Lian's finger hovered over the command, her mind racing as she weighed the implications. Activating the override would disable Voss-Corp's entire surveillance network, crippling the corporation's ability to monitor and control. It would be a blow that Voss might never recover from.

But before she could execute the command, the screens flickered, and a cold, familiar voice echoed through the room.

"Lian Cheng. I expected nothing less from you."

The screen flashed with Elias Voss's face, his expression one of grim satisfaction. He regarded her with a gaze that was both condescending and coldly amused, as though he were watching a predictable game play out exactly as he had planned.

"Do you really think a single command will bring down my empire?" Voss asked, his voice dripping with disdain. "You misunderstand the nature of control. It is not the machines, nor the algorithms. Control lies in perception, in belief. I own the minds of those who depend on me. The data is merely a tool."

Lian met his gaze, her voice steady. "Your control ends here, Voss. The people have seen the truth. They're not going to let you rewrite history anymore."

Voss's expression remained unperturbed. "You forget, Ms. Cheng, that history is written by the victors. And I have no intention of losing."

With a flick of his wrist, he activated an alert, and the room filled with red warning lights. The AI sentries stationed in the hallways came to life, their footsteps echoing through the corridors as they converged on the Heart of Control. She could hear them drawing closer, each step a countdown to her inevitable confrontation.

"You are a footnote, Ms. Cheng," Voss continued, his voice growing colder. "A mere distraction in the grand narrative I have created. When the people see you fail, they will return to my protection. They will forget this resistance, just as they have forgotten so many others before it."

Lian's hand tightened on the console, her mind racing as she considered her options. The override was ready, the system vulnerable. But Voss was right about one thing: a single act would not dismantle the empire he had built, not unless it reached beyond the walls of this building, beyond the screens in front of her.

She took a deep breath, her resolve hardening as an idea formed. Instead of initiating the override, she accessed the network's broadcast system, activating the mainframe's visual and audio feeds. If she could broadcast her message—if she could show the people what lay within the Heart of Control—they would see the truth for themselves.

She pressed the command, and Voss's face flickered with a hint of surprise as he realized what she was doing. "You—what are you—"

His voice was cut off as the broadcast system activated, transmitting live footage from the Heart of Control to every screen in New Hong Kong. Across the city, people stopped in their tracks, watching as Lian Cheng appeared on their devices, her face resolute as she faced down the empire that had oppressed them for so long.

"This is Lian Cheng," she began, her voice steady and clear. "For years, VossCorp has controlled our lives, erased our memories, and manipulated our histories. But today, that ends. I'm here inside the Heart of Control, where Voss has kept his secrets, where he has shaped our past to fit his version of reality."

She tapped a command, displaying files on behavioral conditioning, memory recalibration, and Operation Compliance, each one flashing across the screen for the people to see.

"Look at what he's done," she continued, her voice rising with conviction. "He has erased entire lives, rewritten our thoughts, controlled our every move. But no more. The truth is here, and it's time we take back our freedom."

Outside, the streets erupted in cries of anger, of defiance, the people galvanized by her words. Voss's image flickered across the screen, his face twisted in rage as he struggled to cut the broadcast, his commands failing against the override Lian had embedded.

The sentries burst into the room, their weapons trained on her, but she stood her ground, facing them with unyielding resolve.

"Your reign ends here, Voss," she said, her voice steady as she met the gaze of her oppressors. "And this time, the people will remember."

As the sentries closed in, the screens across New Hong Kong continued to broadcast the truth, the final blow to Voss's empire delivered not with bullets or force, but with the undeniable power of the truth.

Chapter 15: The Rising Tide

The streets of New Hong Kong surged with life, a powerful current of defiance rippling through the city as people flooded into the squares, alleys, and thoroughfares, their voices raised in a unified chorus of anger and resilience. Across the skyline, the imposing VossCorp towers now loomed as relics of oppression, each window and steel beam a silent witness to the empire's crumbling grip. Lian Cheng's broadcast from the Heart of Control had exposed the dark heart of VossCorp's rule, and the truth had ignited a movement that could no longer be contained.

From the safety of an anonymous crowd, Lian watched as thousands gathered in the city's central square, their faces filled with a potent mix of disbelief and hope. The resistance had prepared for this moment, laying down encrypted communication lines and establishing decentralized networks that VossCorp's weakened surveillance struggled to penetrate. And now, for the first time, the people weren't just watching—they were acting.

Phantom's voice crackled through her earpiece, his excitement barely contained. "Lian, it's working. The broadcast spread beyond New Hong Kong. Resistance groups across Asia and Europe are joining in. This is bigger than we expected—VossCorp's networks are collapsing under the strain of these coordinated protests."

She nodded, a surge of relief and pride flooding through her. "It's happening, Phantom. The people finally see it. They're not afraid anymore."

Cipher's voice joined in, his tone triumphant. "And that's not all. The files you broadcast have sparked a cascade effect. Whistleblowers from within VossCorp are leaking additional intel. Layers of the corporation's corruption are being exposed, from off-the-book experiments to illegal surveillance projects. VossCorp's stock is plummeting, and corporate allies are scrambling to distance themselves."

Lian took a deep breath, feeling the weight of their long journey settle over her. This moment had been hard-won, the result of countless sacrifices, close calls, and painful losses. But now, the tide was turning. The people had taken up the torch, and VossCorp's empire was finally crumbling under the weight of its own deception.

As she moved through the crowd, a woman stepped forward, her eyes filled with gratitude. "You're Lian Cheng, aren't you?" the woman asked, her voice barely a whisper. "You're the one who showed us the truth."

Lian nodded, meeting the woman's gaze. "I only showed you what was already there. The rest is all of you. This change belongs to everyone willing to stand up."

The woman gave a small, reverent smile, clasping Lian's hand briefly before disappearing back into the crowd. All around her, people were sharing Requiem's files, analyzing data, organizing protests, and creating connections across regions, their voices growing stronger and more united with each passing hour.

But even as the resistance's strength surged, Lian knew the fight was not yet over. Voss himself would not go down easily. Despite the corporation's weakening infrastructure, VossCorp still held sway in government circles, and they had yet to unleash their full arsenal in an attempt to regain control.

Phantom's voice interrupted her thoughts, his tone grave. "Lian, I have intel from one of our sources within the government. Voss is moving to invoke a special emergency protocol called *Operation Nightfall*. It's an old contingency designed for precisely this situation—a last-resort effort to restore order by force. It involves deploying paramilitary units and reinstating digital suppression tactics, including outright memory purges."

Her blood ran cold. "Nightfall... he's willing to erase entire memories to keep his hold over the city?"

Cipher responded, his tone dark. "It's more than just erasure. Nightfall is a reset. Voss would wipe entire communities, make them forget everything we've achieved, and rebuild his reality from scratch. This isn't just about controlling information; it's about rewriting the people themselves."

Lian felt a surge of fury, her determination hardening. "We can't let that happen. We need to dismantle Voss's remaining power before he can launch Nightfall. Is there any way to shut down his final reserves?"

"There is," Phantom replied, a hint of hesitation in his voice. "But it's risky. Voss's headquarters has a hidden command hub beneath the city—a place he calls the Citadel. It's where he coordinates his most covert operations and controls high-level protocols like Nightfall. The only way to prevent it is to reach the Citadel and disable the system manually."

Lian took a deep breath, feeling the enormity of the task settle over her. The Citadel was VossCorp's last stronghold, buried beneath layers of security and defenses. If she went in, there was a chance she might not come out. But she knew that this was the final stand. If Voss succeeded with Nightfall, every sacrifice, every risk, every life that had joined the resistance would be erased, rewritten to suit his narrative.

"I'll go," she said, her voice unwavering. "I'll take down Nightfall from within."

Phantom's voice softened, a note of admiration in his tone. "We'll be with you, Lian. Whatever happens, we'll make sure the world remembers."

Cipher chimed in, his usual confidence tempered with something close to reverence. "I'll provide you with a distraction. The resistance will storm VossCorp's headquarters and occupy the main floors. It'll buy you time to reach the Citadel."

Lian nodded, feeling the resolve solidify within her. This was their moment, their chance to dismantle the heart of VossCorp's control and free the city from his grip once and for all.

The descent into the Citadel was unlike anything Lian had faced. The entry point was concealed beneath VossCorp's main tower, hidden behind layers of biometric locks and AI defenses. With Cipher's cloaking device and Phantom's encryption layers, she bypassed the first few levels undetected, but as she moved deeper, she could feel the air grow colder, the silence more oppressive.

The Citadel was a fortress of technology and secrets, its walls lined with servers and displays that glowed with a faint, menacing light. She moved cautiously, every step taking her closer to the command center where the Nightfall protocols were housed. The corridors were patrolled by sentries, their mechanical footsteps echoing through the sterile halls, their scanning lights casting sharp, angular shadows.

At last, she reached the central control room, a vast chamber dominated by a single, towering console. The screens displayed lines of code, commands awaiting activation, each one poised to rewrite reality at Voss's whim. In the dim glow of the displays, she saw a figure standing before the console—Elias Voss himself, his presence imposing, his gaze cold and calculating.

"Ms. Cheng," he said, his voice echoing through the room, smooth and unshaken. "I suppose I should admire your persistence. Few have dared to challenge me this far."

Lian met his gaze, her voice steady. "Your empire ends today, Voss. The people have seen the truth, and they won't go back."

Voss raised an eyebrow, a faint smile tugging at his lips. "The people? The people are malleable, Ms. Cheng. They crave structure, stability. Chaos frightens them, and I offer them a world without uncertainty. That is why they will always choose me."

"They chose freedom over your lies, Voss. And now, they're ready to reclaim their lives," she replied, feeling her resolve harden.

Voss's gaze grew colder. "You are nothing but a spark, Ms. Cheng. And sparks burn out."

With a swift motion, he activated the console, his hand hovering over the final command for Nightfall. "Goodbye, Ms. Cheng. I will erase every trace of your existence. Your rebellion will be a forgotten footnote, another experiment in futility."

But before he could initiate the command, Lian lunged forward, engaging a disruptor device that Cipher had modified for this moment. The disruptor sent a pulse through the console, short-circuiting the system and freezing the Nightfall sequence.

Voss staggered back, his expression contorted with fury. "You think this will stop me?"

Lian faced him, her voice unwavering. "It already has. The people are awake, Voss. They know what you are, and they won't let you take control again."

In a final act of defiance, she activated the console's failsafe, dismantling the Citadel's control and flooding the network with the resistance's message. The screens flashed with images of the resistance's victory, of the files and data that exposed Voss's crimes, of the people rising up against his reign.

As the Citadel's lights dimmed, Lian felt the weight of victory settle over her. Voss's empire was shattered, his final weapon rendered useless. The people of New Hong Kong and beyond would remember this moment, the day they reclaimed their freedom from the grip of a false reality.

In the darkness of the Citadel, surrounded by the echoes of a fallen empire, Lian Cheng knew that the tide had finally turned, that the city and its people were free.

Chapter 16: The Dawn of Freedom

As dawn broke over New Hong Kong, the city buzzed with a sense of renewal, the air filled with the quiet hum of possibility. The crowds that had gathered in the central square the previous night were still there, their faces lit with the glow of collective hope and resolve. Word of Lian Cheng's victory in the Citadel had spread like wildfire, igniting a spark that carried through each district, each corner of the city. For the first time in years, people looked up at the VossCorp towers not with fear, but with a sense of victory—a symbol of a power that no longer held sway over them.

Lian stood at the edge of the square, taking in the sight before her. The city had been transformed. The digital screens that had once broadcast VossCorp's propaganda now displayed messages of unity, of resilience, and of truth. The files she had leaked from the Heart of Control had made their way into every corner of the world, revealing VossCorp's lies, exposing the atrocities hidden under the guise of "compliance."

Phantom and Cipher joined her, their faces lined with exhaustion but lit by the same quiet pride that filled her own heart. Phantom looked over the crowd, a slight smile tugging at the corner of his mouth.

"They did it," he said, his voice soft but filled with wonder. "The people took the truth and made it their own. This... this is something even Voss couldn't control."

Lian nodded, her gaze sweeping over the gathering. "For too long, they were kept in the dark, erased, rewritten. But now, they have a chance to reclaim their lives, to rebuild on their terms."

Cipher chuckled, shaking his head. "And you, Lian. You did what most of us thought impossible. You didn't just expose the truth; you tore down an empire."

She smiled, a quiet, weary smile. "I didn't do it alone. None of this would've happened without all of you, without everyone who took the risk, who stood up, who believed we could be free."

As the morning light grew stronger, casting the city in a golden hue, a figure approached them—an older woman with lines of worry etched across her face. Her eyes met Lian's, a look of profound gratitude softening her expression.

"My son," the woman began, her voice thick with emotion, "he was taken by VossCorp years ago. They erased him from our lives, from our memories. But because of you, I remember him again. I remember his laugh, his dreams. Thank you for giving him back to us."

Lian's chest tightened as she took the woman's hand, her voice barely a whisper. "We all deserve the right to remember, to know who we are, who we've lost. I'm so sorry for your son, but he'll never be forgotten now."

The woman nodded, her eyes brimming with tears, before she turned back into the crowd, her place now among those who would carry the story forward. Lian's heart ached for the lives that had been erased, the families torn apart, but she took solace in knowing that the truth would endure. The city would remember.

Phantom's voice broke through her thoughts. "The fallout from this won't end with New Hong Kong. VossCorp's allies are scrambling to distance themselves, and governments worldwide are opening investigations. We've started something unstoppable."

Cipher added, a note of mischief in his voice, "They're even talking about setting up new data laws. Imagine that—the very structure Voss tried to control is being rewritten in response to the truth we released."

But even as the city celebrated, a sense of somber responsibility lingered in Lian's heart. The journey here had come at a steep cost—lives lost, scars left in the wake of battle. But she knew that the dawn of freedom was always born from sacrifice.

Together, they made their way toward the old data exchange, where resistance leaders and representatives from different regions were gathering to discuss the future. As they entered the building, Lian noticed faces she recognized from her journey—figures who had risked everything to stand beside her, to fight for a world where truth and freedom prevailed.

At the head of the room, a young woman named Mira, one of the leaders from New Cairo's resistance cell, stepped forward, her voice strong and filled with conviction.

"We're here because we saw the truth, because we chose to rise up," she began, addressing the room. "The power that held us captive, that tried to rewrite us, has been shattered. But our work isn't over. We need to ensure that no one can ever take that freedom away again."

Lian felt a surge of pride as she listened, watching as the leaders discussed plans to dismantle the remaining structures of VossCorp, to set up networks of transparency and accountability that would prevent the kind of control Voss had wielded.

Phantom leaned in, his voice quiet. "They're laying the foundation for a new world, one that won't let history repeat itself."

Lian nodded, her heart filled with a quiet, fierce determination. "It's time we build something better, something that doesn't rely on fear or lies."

Cipher grinned. "And you, Lian? What's next for you? Are you ready to rest?"

She took a deep breath, glancing around at the faces in the room, at the city she had helped to free. "Maybe," she said, a soft smile playing on her lips. "But only once I know that what we've started here will last."

As the meeting continued, Lian slipped away, stepping outside to take in the city as the sun climbed higher, bathing New Hong Kong in a warm, golden light. The towers of VossCorp still stood, but they no longer cast shadows of fear. They were symbols now, reminders of a past that the city had left behind, relics of a broken empire.

A new dawn had arrived, and with it, the hope of a world where memories were cherished, where truth was honored, and where freedom reigned. For the first time, Lian allowed herself to imagine a future unbound by control, a future that belonged to the people she had fought so hard to protect.

And as the city came alive around her, Lian Cheng knew that their journey was only beginning. The fight for freedom would endure, passed down through stories, through memories, through lives lived openly and honestly. The dawn of freedom had risen, and it would not fade.

Epilogue: The Fractured Code

Months had passed since the dawn of freedom over New Hong Kong, and the world had begun to reshape itself in the wake of VossCorp's downfall. Governments and institutions once bound by Voss's influence now scrambled to rebuild, pledging to honor the principles of transparency and autonomy that the resistance had fought so hard to secure. Across the globe, monuments of surveillance were dismantled, replaced by memorials that honored the lives lost, the identities erased, and the histories rewritten under the shadow of Project Requiem.

Lian Cheng stood atop a hill overlooking the city, the towers of VossCorp still visible in the distance but stripped of their former power. In their place, a new skyline was emerging—symbols of resilience, of a city reclaimed by its people. She took a deep breath, the cool air filled with the hum of life below, the quiet resolve of a world finally free.

Phantom's voice came softly through her earpiece. Even though the resistance had disbanded as an organized force, they still kept in touch, scattered across continents but forever connected by the memory of what they had achieved together.

"You still up there, Lian?" he asked, his voice carrying a warmth she'd come to rely on.

"Just saying goodbye," she replied, a soft smile playing on her lips. "It's strange, isn't it? After everything, it's over. The city's finally free."

Phantom's voice softened. "It's a testament to everything you did, to everyone who believed that change was possible. And now, we're left with the most challenging part: keeping that freedom alive."

She nodded, feeling the weight of his words. "How's Cipher?"

"Doing well. He's in New Moscow, helping set up digital networks designed to preserve unfiltered information—a kind of digital library that VossCorp can't touch, a place where people can keep their histories intact."

She chuckled, imagining Cipher's wiry form hunched over keyboards, his fingers flying as he poured his energy into preserving the truth they had fought so hard to defend. "Of course he is. He was never one to sit still."

They fell into a comfortable silence, each lost in the quiet satisfaction of knowing they had played a part in reshaping the world. But as they stood on the brink of this new era, a question lingered in her mind.

"What do you think happens now, Phantom?" she asked, her voice barely a whisper. "Do we just... go back to our lives?"

Phantom paused, then responded, his tone thoughtful. "I don't think we can ever go back. But maybe that's the beauty of it. We're free to move forward, to rebuild, to live without the shadow of control hanging over us. That's the gift we've given ourselves and everyone else."

She closed her eyes, letting the words sink in, the peace of the moment settling over her like a soft blanket. For the first time in years, the weight of fear, of responsibility, felt lighter, almost bearable.

Phantom's voice came back, a bit hesitant. "Lian... have you ever thought about writing it all down? Your story, the journey, everything you saw and felt? People will remember, but it could help them understand—truly understand—what it took to get here."

A small smile tugged at her lips. "Maybe," she replied, her tone thoughtful. "But not to glorify anything. If I write it, it'll be for everyone who risked everything, for those who lost their lives, who were erased. So that they're never forgotten."

"Exactly," Phantom agreed, his voice filled with quiet pride. "Your story is their story. A testament to a world that dared to resist."

As the sun began to set, casting the city in hues of gold and purple, Lian felt the deep, abiding sense of closure that had eluded her for so long. She had done what she set out to do, and the world would remember. Not through monuments or statues, but in the lives of the people who now lived without fear, without lies.

In her hand, she held a small, worn notebook—the one she'd carried with her since the beginning, filled with encrypted notes, sketches, and fragments of the journey. She opened it, glancing at the first line she'd written so many months ago: *Truth is a beacon, and those who seek it are never truly lost.*

Closing the notebook, she took a final look at the city below, the echoes of Requiem fading into memory, into a story that would be told and retold, reshaped by each new generation. She knew that her work was done, and for the first time, she felt free to let go.

As she walked down the hill, she thought of all those who had walked beside her, each step a testament to their strength, their resilience. And she knew that the world they had reclaimed would carry forward, a beacon of truth that would shine for generations to come.

With a deep breath, she left the past behind, stepping into a future she had helped to shape, a world built on truth, memory, and freedom.